Make or Break Spring

Janet McNaughton

Tuckamore Books
a Creative Publishers imprint
St. John's, Newfoundland
1998

THE CANADA COUNCIL | LE CONSEIL DES ARTS
FOR THE ARTS | DU CANADA
SINCE 1957 | DEPUIS 1957

We acknowledge the support of The Canada Council for the Arts
for our publishing program.

The publisher acknowledges the support of the
Department of Canadian Heritage.

Cover art Jennifer Pohl.

∝ Printed on acid-free paper

Published by
TUCKAMORE BOOKS
An imprint of CREATIVE BOOK PUBLISHING
a division of 10366 Newfoundland Limited
a Robinson-Blackmore Printing & Publishing associated company
P.O. Box 8660, St. John's, Newfoundland A1B 3T7

First printing May 1998
Second printing October 1998

Printed in Canada by:
Robinson-Blackmore Printing & Publishing

Canadian Cataloguing in Publication Data

McNaughton, Janet Elizabeth, 1953-

Make or break spring

Sequel to: Catch me once, catch me twice

ISBN 1-895387-93-0

I. Title.

PS8575.N385M35 1998   jc813'.54   C98-950094-2
PZ7.M23257Ma 1998

Dedication:
For Bernice Morgan and Helen Porter,
who were there in the background,
watching and becoming writers.

Acknowledgments

When I wrote *Catch Me Once, Catch Me Twice*, I did not have a sequel in mind. Many aspects of Ev's life were unresolved at the end of that book because life rarely ties anything up neatly. So, I suppose I must first thank all those readers who requested, and sometimes demanded, a sequel.

Bernice Morgan and Helen Porter were young girls in St. John's during World War II. Both provided valuable information as writers, editors and participants in that time. Members of the Newfoundland Writers' Guild read and offered their comments on one chapter of this book, and I greatly appreciate their input as well. I thank Becky Vogan for her editorial guidance, Don Morgan, my publisher, for always treating me like an adult, and allowing me creative independence, and Jennifer Pohl, the cover artist, for her willingness to collaborate on a cover concept, and her remarkable talent.

Closer to home, I thank my husband Michael, for never complaining about my small contribution to the household income or my neglect of household duties. I thank my daughter Elizabeth for bringing the outside world home to me every day, and for her exuberance for life. And finally, I thank the powers that be for allowing me to run aground in this harbour town where I live among so many talented writers, and writing is regarded as a serious occupation.

Chapter One

A New Day

Peter Tilley glanced at the submarine net as his boat steamed past the Narrows. His imagination dipped below the water's surface to find a dark form, swift and deadly—a German U-boat. The vision was so perfect, he almost gasped for air, couldn't quite convince his pounding heart that he was safe in his own boat. For six long years, those submarines had prowled the North Atlantic just beyond the net that spanned the mouth of St. John's harbour. Taking boats. Taking lives. Shadowing the thoughts and dreams of every man, woman and child in Newfoundland. Now, the power behind them was crumbling to dust. But the U-boats themselves, where were they? Out there still, no doubt. He patted the gunwale of his boat as if to reassure himself. No enemy submarine would sink this vessel. Not now.

Peter had lived on the edge of St. John's harbour for all of his seventeen years. He knew this sheltered bowl of rock and saltwater as well as he knew his own bedroom. Nothing had changed since yesterday. The grey rock hills still sheltered the harbour from the North Atlantic winds. The same white gulls glided in and out of the fog that blanketed everything and tried to hold back spring. Nothing changed, but everything was different. A weight of darkness was lifted from the world. The war was ending.

Crossing from the Battery to the South Side, the prow of Peter's boat stirred the water into thick, lazy rolls until he could imagine he was sailing through pure molasses. This was the first boat Peter had built alone, a twenty-eight foot trap skiff, white with red trim. Her name, the *Evelyn's Pride*, was painted across her prow in black. Peter had taken a tormenting for the name, but that didn't bother him. The boat moved so effortlessly, he almost believed she could find her way across the harbour without him. The make-and-break engine chugged solidly in the engine housing in front of him. It was more than twenty years old, but as reliable as ever. Uncle Ches Barrett, the old boat builder who taught Peter his skill, left this engine to Peter when he died last fall. His final gift. This boat would only be Peter's until he could sell it, but for now, it made him feel like master of the harbour. Master of the harbour, at the beginning of a new day, at the dawn of a new world. The words fell into the make-and-break's rhythmic chug. There never was a better day than this, May 2, 1945.

The trip from the Battery to the South Side was not long. Almost too soon, Peter cut the engine and tied his boat to a wooden wharf. He scrambled up a short ladder, carrying his book bag and his cane, shouldered the bag, then limped past the warehouses to South Side Road. The cane, unneeded in the boat, was a necessity now. He was well accustomed to his uneven gait, but never left the water without regret. Out there, his handicap didn't slow him.

Peter passed the Long Bridge that crossed the Waterford River. He was now "above the bridge" in St. John's parlance. The maze of old houses, coal depots, warehouses and cooperages below the bridge gave way here to larger, fine-looking houses facing the rail yard. Ahead, his friend Evelyn sat on the front steps of a house. She was two years younger than Peter, tall and slender, with a small, sharp face and a mop of dark, curly hair. On her lap sat her brother, a fair-haired boy of two and a half. He was christened Chesley Ian, after the old boat builder and his grandfather. But the resemblance to his grandfather was so strong that Ian quickly became his name. In spite of the difference in their ages, Ev and Ian were deep in conversation. Even at a distance, Peter saw how Ev's tall body shaped itself around the child, as if to protect him from all harm.

When Ian noticed Peter, he jumped off Ev's lap. Ev grabbed him by the wrist before he could dart out into the road.

"Peter!" Ian greeted him with joy. Peter smiled down on him.

"Morning, Ian," Peter said. "Morning, Ev." He could tell from Ev's face that she had not yet heard the news. "You didn't listen to the radio this morning, did you?"

She shook her head. "It's Mum's day off. We didn't want to wake her."

Leaning heavily on his cane, Peter lowered himself until he was eye to eye with Ian. "Well, Ian, I'll tell you a great bit of news. Hitler's dead."

Ian looked back at his sister, uncertain.

"He doesn't understand, Peter," Ev said. She squatted in front of her little brother. "Hitler was a bad man. He's gone now, Ian. He can't ever hurt anyone again." She took Ian in her arms and looked at Peter over her little brother's head. Her eyes filled with tears. "Then it's true? The war is really over?"

Peter nodded. "Just a matter of time."

"Maybe now my father will come home," Ev said. Her father had been missing overseas since just before Ian was born.

A car pulled up beside the house, intruding.

Peter was surprised. "Where's your grandfather?" he said.

Ev spoke quickly before the car door opened. "He phoned last night to say he couldn't come. I asked Grandpa not to send *him*." She spat the last word out, then fell silent.

The man who stepped from the car was small and compact. His tweed suit was well-made, but old and rumpled. His sandy hair was barely touched with grey, and his face was lined with kindly concern. He looked directly at Ev, cautious and uncertain. Then, as if setting himself a difficult task, said, "Good morning, Evelyn."

Ev only nodded, but Ian squirmed from her arms and ran towards this man.

"Doctor T'orn, Doctor T'orn," Ian cried. Relief showed in the man's smile as he scooped little Ian into his arms. Then he stood looking at Ev and Peter across the child's head, just as Ev had held Ian only moments before.

As Peter watched, Ev's body assumed a fighter's stance, chin up, hands clenched at her sides as if they would come up as fists at any moment. She could not have known how she looked—as if she wanted to wrestle her brother out of this man's arms.

Doctor Thorne's gaze shifted uncertainly from Ev's face to Peter, then back to Ev. "Your grandfather asked me to drive you to school today," he said, offering an explanation he must have known was not needed.

4

"Ian," Ev spoke so sharply that her brother startled. "Ian," she said again more gently, "I have to go to school now. Say goodbye to Doctor Thorne and I'll take you inside."

Ian planted a resounding kiss on John Thorne's cheek. Ev winced at the delight on the doctor's face. He set Ian down and tousled the child's silky blond hair. "Be good, Ian," he said.

Ev shot him a scornful glance. "He's always good," she said as she took her brother's hand and led him into the house.

Just before he disappeared through the door, Ian turned back to Peter. "Ian want boat ride," he said.

"After school if the weather allows, Ian," Peter said. Then Ev and Ian were gone.

In her wake, Ev left an awkward silence. Peter tried to think of something to say. He had no quarrel with John Thorne himself. In fact, he liked this awkward bachelor doctor who had a reputation for secret acts of charity.

John Thorne wasn't one for small talk, but today he said, "The house could use a coat of paint. Perhaps I'll have someone see to it when the weather settles."

"Whenever that might be." Peter laughed. April had been rainy and dark. As far as he could see, the dark green paint on the fine three-storey house was perfect. John Thorne looked so intently, Peter thought he was studying the paint, until he noticed the doctor was staring fixedly at the window of Ev's mother's bedroom, and had not looked anywhere else.

From the gossip (and there was plenty), Peter knew John Thorne had never looked at a woman until Ev's mother went back to nursing school. The doctor was now so painfully smitten that Peter could only feel sympathy, something he took care to hide from Ev.

It would be better, Peter decided, if Ev found John Thorne looking elsewhere when she returned. So he spoke. "It's a fine house, Doctor Thorne. Did you always live here?"

"All my life until I went away to medical school at McGill, and the year after that, when I worked with the Grenfell Mission, on the Labrador. What a country that is, Peter! So wild and open. I loved it." Just briefly, Peter caught a glimpse of a younger man who had found his place in life as a medical missionary in Labrador.

"But you came back," Peter said.

"Yes. I came back. My father died, you see, and Mother didn't like to be alone. So I came back, took over Father's practice, and lived in this house with Mother again, until she died last year." Peter knew the doctor was talking about twenty years of his life. The regret in his voice made Peter understand what a sacrifice this must have been, but Doctor Thorne quickly pulled himself back to the present, becoming again the awkward man Peter knew. "And then, well, the house was too big for me, and Nina, um, Mrs. McCallum, that is to say *Nurse* McCallum, well, she was ready to live away from Evelyn's grandparents, and she, being widowed, well, not exactly widowed—" His voice trailed off. No one ever openly suggested Ev's father was dead. A shockwave of silence followed the exposed truth.

Ev stepped out into that silence, opened the back door of the doctor's car and climbed in without speaking. Peter wondered if she'd overheard. Ev refused to believe her father might be dead.

Peter gave the doctor a small, sympathetic nod. "We'll be late if we don't get a move on."

John Thorne cast one quick glance back at Nina McCallum's window, then walked to the car with Peter. The doctor made a U-turn back towards the main part of the city on the opposite side of the river, and drove across the same Long Bridge Peter had passed shortly before. There, Peter noticed a small, sharp-faced soldier, wearing the khaki-coloured uniform that identified Newfoundlanders who fought in the British artillery units overseas. The soldier gave them a startled look, then quickly averted his eyes. That look caught Peter's attention. Who was this man? No one Peter recognized. And why would he look like that? It didn't make sense.

Peter tried to keep a conversation going on the way to school. "What do you suppose will happen to Newfoundland now that the war is over, Doctor Thorne?"

"Oh, that's hard to say, Peter. I've never bothered much with politics. You'd have to ask Doctor McCallum." Ev's grandfather, the elder Ian McCallum, was a highly respected doctor. Peter noticed that no one seemed to respect him more than John Thorne. It would not have been easy to talk with Doctor Thorne at the best of times, but now, with Evelyn radiating cold silence from the back seat, it was impossible. The conversation faltered. Luckily, the trip was brief.

Peter was glad to escape the tension of the car when he climbed back into the cool spring morning. "Thank you, Doctor Thorne," he said. Ev joined him silently.

"No trouble at all, Peter." Doctor Thorne hesitated. "Will you need a drive home?"

Peter glanced at Ev. "No, thanks. It's all downhill. I think I can make it on my own steam."

As John Thorne's car disappeared towards the hospital, Peter turned to Evelyn. His annoyance at her behaviour surprised him. "He's not a bad sort, Ev," he said. "You could like him if you tried."

Peter expected an explosion of anger, but it didn't come. Instead, Ev spoke evenly. "If he's not a bad sort, why is he chasing after a married woman? He didn't have to move out of that house after his mother died. The rent is a joke. He acts surprised to see it every month. It's just an excuse to get closer to my mother. And you saw how Ian is with him. Peter, it's like my father's disappearing." There was more than anger in her eyes, something closer to anguish.

Peter's annoyance vanished. "I'm sorry, Ev," he said gently. "Now that the war is over…"

"Do you think he'll come home?" There was a pleading tone in her voice he'd never heard before.

Peter knew what she wanted him to say, but he couldn't. "Maybe now you'll find out what happened to him." That was the best he could do. The school bell rang and Peter gave Ev's arm a quick pat before they went to the separate doors marked "Boys" and "Girls."

There wasn't a hope that Duncan McCallum was still alive, Peter felt sure. In the two and a half years since the telegram had announced he was missing, they'd never had a word to say what had happened to him. Someday, finally, Peter hoped Ev might accept the idea her father wasn't coming home. But she wasn't ready yet.

Chapter Two

The Scholarship

As soon as Ev entered the classroom, Miss Gould looked up. "Evelyn McCallum, don't even bother to sit down. Straight to the principal's office." Miss Gould was always abrupt, but this command took Ev by surprise.

A nervous giggle rippled through the class as forty-three girls turned to stare. Some looked horrified, some looked smug. Miss Gould smiled at Ev. "Don't look so worried. You're no angel, but I don't suppose they'll hang you. Off you go."

A chorus of excited whispers followed Ev into the hall. She was glad to escape. Prince of Wales College was different from their junior school. Here, boys and girls studied in separate classes, except for subjects hardly anyone took, like Latin and chemistry. Ev found the all-girl classes hard to bear. They seemed to bring out the worst in the girls—giggling, gossip, backbiting. She knew Peter felt the same way about his classes. The boys were more aggressive, more likely to bully. In the mixed classes at their old school, the boys and girls had somehow balanced each other out.

Ev was surprised to find Peter outside the principal's office. "Any idea what we did?" she whispered.

"No. I thought we were too busy for trouble." It was true. Peter had been allowed to do extra schoolwork to make up

9

for time he'd lost to the illness that had left him crippled years before. Ev only helped Peter to study at first, but it soon became clear that she could do the work too. For the past two years, they'd progressed together at their own speed. While everyone else was busy with sports or movies or dating, schoolwork became the focus of their lives, almost a game they played together. It set them apart. "Brains," everyone called them, even to their faces. But that didn't matter. They hadn't needed other friends.

Mr. Warren, the principal, was ancient and stern. Called out of retirement because of the war, he had even taught some of the grandparents of his current pupils. Never a big man, he now seemed shrunken with age inside his suit. But he still commanded respect like no one else. He smiled when he saw Evelyn and Peter, and the knot of tension in Ev's chest undid a little. There was no anger in his face.

"Well, here are our two scholars. Sit down." He waved them into some hard wooden chairs in front of his desk. "How's your grandmother, Peter?"

"She's fine, sir."

"Did I ever tell you she helped my wife when my oldest son was born?"

Peter nodded. It was all Ev could do to keep from laughing. Mr. Warren said exactly the same thing every time he saw Peter. Mrs. Bursey, Peter's grandmother, must have helped every mother in St. John's in childbirth at one time or another.

"Well now," Mr. Warren said, "we'll just wait for young Dawe." The clock on the office wall ticked the seconds off methodically in the silence that followed. Stan Dawe. Why hadn't Ev worn her new blouse? Was her skirt wrinkled? She wanted to straighten her uniform, but couldn't in front of Peter and Mr. Warren. She fidgeted instead.

The Dawes were a family of coal merchants. Knowing that, Ev might have expected Stan to be small and dark, grubby with coal dust. Well, he wasn't tall, but his wavy blond hair, even teeth and fair skin never looked grubby. He was a track and field star, muscular and broad shouldered. But it was his sensitive-looking face that made most of the girls in Ev's school weak in the knees. The girls thought he looked like Leslie Howard, the British actor who had played Ashley Wilkes in *Gone with the Wind*. The actor had died in the war when his transport plane crashed in 1943. Somehow, irrationally, this tragic death added to Stan's allure.

Ev knew how many girls in her class would trade a month's worth of chocolate mice to be sitting in her place. But the idea of seeing Stan in this small space made her break into a cold sweat. She was still wishing she'd taken more care with her appearance when the office door flew open, and there he was. Ev's heart tried to escape through her mouth. She almost choked with embarrassment. Peter gave her a look of disbelief, but Stan simply smiled. Behind his smile was a knowing conceit that almost made Ev hate him. Almost, but not quite.

He turned to Mr. Warren. "I'm sorry, sir," he said. "I was at track practice."

"Never mind that, Dawe. Sit down," Mr. Warren said. "Now, I suppose you're wondering why I called you all here today." He chuckled dryly at his own small joke. He sounded like someone in *Secrets of Scotland Yard*. "Well, as I'm sure you know, a scholarship has been established in Duncan McCallum's name." He nodded towards Ev with something approaching sympathy. "Your father, Evelyn, was one of the best students ever to pass through this school. I taught him myself.

"Each year, the scholarship will send one graduate of PWC to McGill to study engineering. It's to be awarded for the first time in a few weeks." His voice softened a little. "Now that the war is ending, that's fitting." Then he continued in his usual brusque manner. "You three are the main contenders, and I just want to say this: there may be gossip that Evelyn is only on the list because of her father. That's foolishness and I want you all to know it. Evelyn McCallum's name appears on this list because of her academic achievement and for no other reason. It that clear?"

"Yes, Mr. Warren," they mumbled in unison. For the second time that morning, Ev wondered if it were possible to die of embarrassment.

"Good. I'm glad we have that out of the way. Now, before we go any further, we need to know if all of you are actually interested in studying engineering. The committee doesn't want to waste its time."

Stan spoke first. Somehow, Evelyn knew he would. Still, she could not force herself to look away from his handsome face.

"I'm extremely interested in pursuing a career in engineering, sir," he said.

Mr. Warren smiled, then turned to Peter. For as long as Ev had known him, Peter had been interested in building things, discovering how best to put them together. He was born to be an engineer, but Peter's family was not rich. This scholarship would ensure his future. All this must have passed through Peter's mind too, but he only nodded and said, "Yes, sir, I'm glad to be considered."

And then it was Ev's turn. I'm only fifteen, she thought. I shouldn't have to make up my mind about a career so soon. But this scholarship was for her father's sake. She wanted to make him proud. How would Peter feel, though, if she spoiled his chances? Ev looked at him. He smiled and nodded his head slightly, encouraging her to say yes. Then she glanced at Stan. His lips curled into a tight smirk. He didn't think she could win. That did it. "Yes," Ev said in a rush. "Yes, sir. I would like to be considered for the scholarship. Thank you."

The smirk fell from Stan Dawe's face. Peter beamed at her.

"Well, then. The three of you are about equal in academic standing, so the committee has decided to set an exam. The one who scores the highest will be this year's winner. The exam will take place in a few weeks, and the award will be presented the next day."

By recess, even girls who were not in her class knew something was up. Ev braced herself for their questions as they walked across the street and down the hill to Snow's store. Peter always stayed up by the school with the boys. It was just too awkward to spend recesses with him. Outside the store, a crowd surrounded Ev. "What happened, Ev?" Doris Piercy asked. "Was Old Man Warren mad at you for something?"

"No, nothing like that," Ev said. But a dozen curious faces continued to stare. "It was about the scholarship—the one for my father."

"Oh, they want you to present it to the winner, I bet." That was Letty Winsor.

"No, they want to know if I'm applying. There's an exam."

That silenced Letty as Ev hoped it would.

"Who else, Ev?" another girl asked.

"Peter Tilley."

"Figures. All brains, that one..."

"And Stan Dawe."

"Stan Dawe!" a chorus cried.

"You were *alone* with Stan Dawe?"

"Don't be so foolish, Violet. They was in the principal's office." Pansy Green tossed her black curls, not bothering to hide her scorn.

"Oh, he's some handsome. I'd die to be alone with Stan Dawe," Violet Harvey continued as if she hadn't heard.

Ev groped for a change of topic. "Hitler's dead," she said.

"Yes, and it'll be V-E Day any time now."

"What's that stand for, V-E Day?"

"Have you no brains at all, Vi? Victory in Europe is what it stands for, 'cause we're still fighting Japan."

"Well, Pansy Green, you're such a Miss Know-it-all. When's it going to be then?"

Pansy paused. "I don't know. No one does. They're waiting for the Nazis to give in. But the war's as good as over. My uncle says the boys will be coming home now."

There was an uncomfortable silence. Ev realized everyone was looking at her again.

Then Letty spoke. "Saw you getting out of Doctor Thorne's car this morning, Ev. Visiting your mom, was he?"

Several girls sniggered. Ev knew a display of temper was

exactly what Letty wanted, so she struggled to stay calm. "No, he wasn't. My grandfather asked him to bring Peter and me to school on his way to the hospital." Her tone was even but she felt her cheeks burn.

"Well," Pansy said, "they aren't saying anything about ending the blackout. When the lights go on again all over the world, Newfoundland'll still be sitting in the dark. And V-E Day is supposed to be quiet as a funeral. I think there should be a big parade, fireworks and dances. What do you think, Doris?"

Ev looked at her in surprise. Pansy had deliberately drawn the girls' attention away from Ev. She wasn't sure what to make of Pansy. She looked older than sixteen. Even the lumpy school uniform could not disguise her beauty. In spite of her outport speech, which she made no attempt to correct, Pansy moved in the rarefied atmosphere of the very popular. Ev was almost a social outcast in comparison, but Pansy was always friendly with her. Ev wondered why. They didn't have much in common. Could she possibly want Ev's help with schoolwork? As they walked back up the hill, Ev shrugged. She was grateful to Pansy. If Pansy wanted something, she'd let Ev know.

Ev waited outside the school for Peter at the end of the day. Because of his leg, he was almost always the last one out. The illness and operation that had ruined his knee came before Ev knew him. It was hard for her to imagine him any other way.

She smiled when she saw him limping towards her. Peter was such a steadfast feature in her life that she seldom really looked at him. Now, she surprised herself. No one swooned after Peter, but his straight, chestnut-coloured hair and warm brown eyes made him just as handsome as Stan Dawe in his way. "Thanks for saying we'd walk home this morning," she said. She didn't elaborate—she avoided Doctor Thorne's name whenever possible.

"Well, if it wasn't for me, you wouldn't have had to face Doctor Thorne this morning," he said. It was true. Ev's grandfather drove them both to school for Peter's sake.

Peter looked up at the grey sky. "It's not a bad day. No rain, hardly any fog, no wind. I'd just as soon walk."

"Just as soon walk as put up with my bad temper, you mean," Ev joked as they started towards the harbour.

Peter grinned. "Well, there is that."

Ev sighed. "It's not just him, Peter. The gossip is the worst part. Letty was at me today." She repeated the conversation at recess. "If Pansy Green hadn't changed the subject, I'd have lost my temper altogether."

"Pansy Green," Peter said. "Where's she come from? Do you know?"

"Oh, somewhere out around the bay," Ev said. She hadn't intended to start a conversation about Pansy.

"I hear her father is a district magistrate," Peter continued.

Ev looked at him. "You have some particular interest in Pansy Green?"

She expected him to deny it or make a joke, but he only blushed. Ev didn't give herself time to consider what this might mean, rushing on to cover her embarrassment. "Anyway, Letty isn't the only one who's saying things. I bet you've heard talk too."

Peter didn't deny it. "Some women tried gossiping to

Nan. She put them in their place right quick. But you know how people are, Ev. Your mom's a decent woman. It's only idle gossip."

"Maybe."

"You don't mean that."

"Not about my mother. I'm thinking of him. If he'd just leave us alone."

"But Ev" — Peter's voice was gentle and cautious— "your mom's happier now that she's got something like a place of her own, wouldn't you say? Doctor Thorne's been good for her, in his way."

Ev said nothing. Peter had the most annoying habit of complete honesty. Why couldn't he just take her side the way he was supposed to?

"She's a good mother, Ev," he continued. "She's working hard to upgrade her nurse's training so she can provide for you and Ian. Getting out from under your grandmother's thumb has done her some good. I never heard her laugh until she moved into the Thorne place. I'd say that's worth a little gossip."

Ev sighed. "Okay, you're right. I'm selfish. I want her to myself. I want Ian to myself. I want my father back. The war is over. Everything is supposed to go back to normal now."

"Ev, the war's over, but I don't think things will ever be the same."

Ev said nothing. It was true, but that didn't make it any easier to accept. They walked on in silence.

"I thought you showed Stan Dawe today," Peter said after a while. The admiration in his voice warmed her.

"He's full of himself, that one." It felt slightly dishonest to talk about Stan that way when he could make her heart pound, but she knew that was what Peter wanted to hear.

"I wonder why he's even here," Peter said. The bitterness in his voice surprised her. "I mean, most of them merchant princes gets shipped off to private schools in Canada."

"Oh, he's supposed to be learning the family business."

Peter raised his eyebrows. His look said, "How would you know?" as clearly as if he'd spoken.

Now it was Ev's turn to blush. "Some girls never stop talking about him. Like Violet Harvey," she added to deflect his attention.

"Well, I hope you beat him to that scholarship," Peter said with fervour.

Ev decided to be perfectly honest. "What about you? You need the money more than Stan or me, Peter."

"That's what the *Evelyn's Pride* is for," Peter said. He'd built the boat to sell to a returning serviceman. The money would help pay for his education.

"You shouldn't have to sell that boat. And anyway, it might not be enough. Will your father help you?"

"He always has. And Nan's got some money put aside for me."

Ev hesitated. "Will your father come home now?"

"I don't know. I guess he'll stay on in Argentia, given the chance." Peter's father had gone to work on the American base at Argentia at the beginning of the war. Peter and his grandmother had lived alone ever since, rarely seeing his father.

When they came to the Long Bridge, they stopped. Ev stared idly into the sluggish brown river until her own reflection suddenly came into focus, hideously distorted by whorls and eddies in the muddy water. It looked like the face of someone drowned. For a second, Ev was gripped by a horrible fascination. Then she pulled away, shaking herself to break the spell.

Peter had noticed nothing. "Don't let me stop you from trying for this scholarship, Ev," he said. "Just do the best you can. I'll take care of myself." He spoke without anger or resentment.

Ev glanced back into the water. The terrible reflection was gone. She turned to Peter. "Okay. May the best man win."

He grinned. "Proper thing."

Ian sat on the front steps of the Thorne house with Annie, the girl who did the housework. When he saw Ev, he bolted across the street and threw himself at her skirts.

"Ian, you shouldn't run into the road like that!" Ev said picking him up. "See the cars?" A few cars were parked on the road. None were moving. "The cars might not stop, Ian. You could get hurt."

"Oh, Evelyn, there's hardly any traffic around here," Annie said.

Ev reined her temper in. The war had made so many good jobs that hired girls were hard to find. Annie was careless and did nothing unless she was told, but she'd be impossible to replace. "It would only take one car, Annie. He's got to learn." Nothing bad could ever happen to Ian. Ever. "Do you understand, Ian?"

The child nodded. "Boat ride now," he said to Peter as they walked to the house.

Peter laughed. "Maybe after a bit, Ian. I'd rather not start her up till I'm ready to make the trip home. What's that you got in the bowl?" he asked, pointing to the steps.

"Bubble water," Ian said.

"You know how to make bubbles?" Peter asked in mock amazement. Ian nodded proudly.

"No! Well, show me."

"If you're looking after Ian now, your mom wants me to do some ironing," Annie said.

Ev nodded. "Where's Mum?"

Annie jerked her head towards the house. "Inside, scrubbing the house to splinters. As usual on her day off."

Ian settled himself on the bottom step, between the feet of Peter and Ev. "Make bubbles like this, Peter," he said. He dipped a ring of wire into the soapy water, puffed out his cheeks and blew with extreme concentration. A small flotilla of bubbles sailed off on the light breeze. Ian giggled with delight. "See? Make bubbles."

Peter moved down to the bottom step beside Ian. "Can I try?" he asked. Ian nodded and handed Peter the wire loop. Peter studied it. "You could use a pipe for bubbles, you know."

Ian made a face. Ev laughed. "We tried that once. Ian swallowed some bubble water, didn't you?"

Ian nodded.

"What was the bubble water like, Ian?" Peter asked.

Ian struggled to find the right word. "Distasteful," he said finally.

Ev swallowed a laugh, giving Peter a stern look so he would do the same. Ian didn't like to be laughed at.

"I made him the bubble wand so he doesn't need a pipe," she said as soon as she could trust herself to speak.

"So this is your handiwork, is it?" Peter asked. He twisted the piece of wire in his hand.

His scrutiny embarrassed Ev. Peter was a craftsman, and this was a crude piece of work.

As if his thoughts had followed her own, he asked, "Ever carve any more?"

Ev shook her head. "Not since Uncle Ches died. It's different for you. You know what you're doing. I never learned enough."

"You could get better."

"Peter, it's just kid's stuff with me. Anyway, there isn't time now."

Peter didn't argue. He turned to Ian instead. "Let's see how it works then."

Ian and Peter took turns, and sometimes blew together on the count of three. A weak sun peeked out for the first time in days, adding a little warmth to the world. Bubbles rose over South Side Road like liberated rainbows. Ian clapped his hands and laughed. Ev let her troubles go with the bubbles, sunning herself on the steps like a cat. With Ian and Peter, she was almost perfectly happy. The long winter was over. The war was almost over. What stretched ahead seemed like an endless summer. A lifetime of summer.

Across the river stood some warehouses connected with the rail yard. The riverbank was covered with last year's bleached, dead plants. There was no path, and it was unusual for anyone to walk there. But now, Ev noticed a small rabbit-faced soldier. He almost seemed to be watching them. She realized he looked familiar.

"Peter," she said, "see that serviceman across the river? I've seen him before."

Peter stood up. "Ian," he said, "you think Annie's got any bit of cake around for us?"

Ian nodded. "Gingerbread."

"Good. Suppose we go and get some now. All of us." He emphasized the last sentence. Then he took Ian's hand and started up the steps. "I seen that same fellow myself this morning," he said quietly to Ev over his shoulder, so Ian wouldn't hear. Then he added, more loudly, "Better bring that bowl of bubble water."

Ev scooped the bowl of soapy water up, looking back across the river. The young soldier stared directly at her. Neither of them moved for one long moment and, in spite of the warmth of the day, she shivered.

"Ev," Peter called from the door. As Ev swung around, the bowl of soapy water flew from her hand. It didn't break on the newly thawed ground, but the water splashed across Ev's shoes. When she looked back over the river, the soldier was gone.

Chapter Three

The Silent Sirens

As much as Ev disliked Doctor Thorne, she secretly loved his house. A narrow house, connected to its mirror image, it wasn't as big as her grandparents' house, nor anywhere near as neat or clean. Doctor Thorne's mother had died of a lingering illness. For years, she had been cared for by a housekeeper and finally a series of nurses while everything else in the house had been ignored.

As a result, Ev found herself living in a wonderful jumble, some of which dated back to the time when Doctor Thorne's father was a boy. Even though they'd lived here for three months, Ev's mother was still struggling to bring a few rooms up to standard. Most of the house was still a dusty treasure chest. So Ev was not surprised to find her mother with a clean rag tied around her head standing at the top of a ladder, cleaning the dining room light fixture.

"Thank heaven," she said when she saw them. "Dusting won't be enough for these globes. I just decided they need a good washing. Let me hand them down to you, Peter, there's a good chap. You'll save me from going up and down the ladder." Although she'd come to Newfoundland more than twenty years before, she still had a crisp English accent.

Peter willingly took his place beside the ladder. Ev knew he was dazzled by her mother, who had married young and was very pretty. Ian's fair hair and rosy complexion came from her. She was, as Ev's father had said, an English rose—blond with hazel eyes that always seemed to be smiling. Most people liked her instantly, but her mildness sometimes exasperated Ev, especially when they'd lived with Ev's grandparents. Now, in this house, Ev had to admit her mother seemed more independent.

Unlike Ian, Ev had inherited few of her mother's traits. She was pure McCallum, as her father always said, tall, blunt and awkward with people. Ev didn't want to be small and mild like her mother, but she sometimes wished for some of her mother's easy charm.

Ian came to the foot of the ladder. "Where Melodus is?" he asked his mother.

"Just where you left him, Ian. On the bookshelf near the fireplace," she replied without looking down.

Ian went to the fireplace and retrieved his favourite object, a stuffed piping plover, *Melodus Charadrius*. He carried the bird carefully by its base, set it on a table near the couch, then climbed onto the couch to watch his mother work.

Melodus was not a plush toy, but a real stuffed bird. Doctor Thorne's father, the elder Doctor Thorne, had been an amateur taxidermist. His work appeared in unexpected places all over the house. Many of his glass-eyed, stuffed birds and animals were fixed in unusual, almost artistic poses, like the snowy owl on the second floor landing that was poised, wings outstretched, as if to strike a weasel that lay seemingly paralysed with terror beneath it. The effect was wonderful. When they moved into the house, Ian promptly abandoned his teddy bear. He wasn't allowed to take the piping plover outside, but inside the house he carried it everywhere. Ev never knew where it might pop up.

Ev's mother handed down the last of the glass globes, then stepped off the ladder. "Thank you, gallant sir," she said, and curtsied. Peter blushed deeply. It seemed to Ev there was always some male ready to throw himself at her mother's feet. She wasn't meant to be a widow. The thought flashed though Ev's mind unbidden. She pushed it away.

"I'll wash these now," Nina said, collecting the globes from Peter. "Does anyone want a snack?"

"Gingerbread for Peter, please," said Ian from the couch. "Then boat ride."

Ev's mother smiled. "No boat ride today, Ian. Your grandfather's stopping in to see you on his way home. But I'll get you a snack."

"Do you need help?" Peter asked.

"No, thank you, Peter. I'll ask Annie to fix some cake while I wash these."

"No boat ride," Ian said as his mother left the dining room. He sounded disappointed. Then he perked up. "Read book, Peter," he demanded.

"Please," Ev prompted.

"Please and thanks," Ian said.

Peter picked the right book without asking. Ian's other favourite thing in the world was an old two-volume set, *Native Birds and Mammals of North America*, a reference work. The pages of colour plates in the middle of each volume were filled with pictures that looked remarkably like the aging stuffed animals that dotted the house. It occurred to Ev that this wasn't a coincidence. Old Doctor Thorne must have used the pictures for inspiration. Ev's *Winnie-the-Pooh* books could not compete with *Native Birds and Mammals*. Ian would sit in rapt silence listening to lengthy descriptions of the characteristics, range and habits of birds and animals.

"What'll you have today, Ian?" Peter asked.

"Lynx."

Ev smiled. It might be porcupine, raccoon or otter, osprey or red-tailed hawk. Ian always knew exactly which animal or bird he wanted. Ev had done nothing to shorten or simplify the text, hoping at first that Ian would grow tired of the long words and dry descriptions. He didn't. He loved every word, even the Latin names, which was how his plover came to be called Melodus.

Ian curled up beside Peter, the big book covering both their laps. "Lynx. *Lynx canadensis*. The lynx is one of two wild cats native to North America," Peter began.

An only child, Peter was kinder and more patient with Ian than most boys his age would be. Ev sat in a wingback chair facing the couch, watching them. Past Peter and Ian, through the yellowed lace curtains, she could see directly across the river where the soldier had been. He wasn't there now. Ev wondered why Peter had seemed so alarmed, but they couldn't talk about it with Ian near.

Before Peter finished reading about the lynx, the front door opened. "Grandpa!" Ev said. She flew into the hall, Ian close at her heels. They both hugged him at the same time.

"Goodness, children, anyone would think you hadn't seen me for weeks." Their grandfather laughed, but Ev could see how pleased he was.

"Well, we didn't see you this morning," she protested.

Ian tugged on his pant leg. "I want an up." His grandfather swept him off the floor.

"Oh, Father, I thought I heard you." Nina McCallum joined them. "Will you have some tea?" The bond between Nina and her father-in-law had grown since Ev's father had disappeared.

"No, Nina, I can't stay. It looks as if I'll have to go back to the hospital this evening."

"Oh, what a shame. We've hardly seen you at all today."

"Yes, well, that's what Ian and Ev said too. Perhaps I'll stop in for a cup of tea tomorrow morning."

"That would be lovely."

Next morning, when her grandfather came for that cup of tea, Ev was finally able to slip away with Peter so they could talk about the soldier.

"I think we should go to the police," Peter said. "I noticed the same fellow on the Long Bridge yesterday morning. It bothers me, the idea of someone lurking round your house. You know as well as I do the police should have been called the last time. That Gerry would have made away with you, given half a chance."

Ev still felt a chill remembering the American soldier who had threatened her, even though it had happened before Ian was born. "But this is different," she said. "This one doesn't look scary. I'd feel silly calling the police, and I'd rather not upset my mother." She guessed Peter would listen to this last argument if nothing else, and she was right.

"Perhaps it's not right to worry your mom," Peter conceded. "Keep your eyes open though, please, Ev. And let me know if you sees him again."

Ev nodded quickly as her grandfather came out the front door. "Okay. I will."

Every Thursday morning, precisely at 10:00 a.m., the air

raid sirens went off. Every week throughout the war. You could set your watch by them. At 9:58 that morning, Ev and her classmates sat in their desks, waiting. It was useless to start a new geometry problem because the sirens would go off in two minutes. Then everyone would go to the basement until the all-clear sounded. Ev hated the air raid sirens. They had gone off the day she'd first learned her father was missing. Ever after, it seemed to Ev as if they screamed out the pain of the entire war in a language beyond words. She braced herself. 9:59. The clock hit 10:00 with a decisive click.

Nothing happened.

Outside, rain drizzled down. Sparrows hopped from branch to branch in the leafless trees. Silence. The girls looked at one another in disbelief, then burst into excited chatter. Miss Gould didn't stop them. "Another sign the war is almost over," she said, smiling. "Now, you have that much more time to devote to your geometry." The girls groaned, but went back to work cheerfully.

Ev didn't know what to feel. She never wanted to hear those sirens again. Not ever. And yet—if they had stopped, the war was really over. Suddenly, she understood what that meant. All this time, she had been able to believe her father was out there somewhere, only the war had kept him from finding his way home. Now, it was possible he never would. She raised her hand.

"Yes, Evelyn?"

"Please, Miss Gould, may I be excused?" She almost managed to sound normal.

The teacher gave her a puzzled look, but nodded. Ev got up so quickly her geometry book and copy book spilled to the floor. Tears already stung her eyes, so she left the books where they landed and hurried from the classroom, aware that everyone was watching her. She rushed down the empty hall, into the bathroom, thankful to find it empty as well. She pulled a frosted window open and gulped at the cool, damp air as if she were drowning. It's over, she thought. It's over and he isn't coming home. She couldn't catch her breath. Big sobs welled up inside her as she slid to the floor and gave herself over to grief.

Ev was almost cried out when the bathroom door opened. She peeked through her fingers just enough to see a pair of loafers. Good. It wasn't a teacher. She covered her eyes again and sat there, hoping the girl would be too embarrassed to speak.

"Thought I'd find you here," the voice said. It was Pansy Green. Her tone was not gloating or sympathetic, just matter of fact.

"Go away," Ev said into her wrists. Pansy Green! Now she was the embarrassed one. She heard fabric rustle as Pansy crouched to face her. Gentle fingers pried Ev's hands from her face. Ev blinked in the light. Her face felt hot and bloated. "I'd rather be alone, thank you," Ev said. She tried to sound dignified. Given the situation, it wasn't easy.

"No, you wouldn't," Pansy said. She sat down on the floor beside Ev, her back against the wall. She gathered her skirt around her ankles. "Damn uniform," she muttered. "More wrinkles than an old prune." She was silent for a moment, then she spoke. "Mom died when I was twelve," she said.

"Oh."

Pansy sighed. "This isn't something I talks about with just anyone. So don't go repeating what I says. Okay?"

Ev nodded.

"Mom was always after helping someone out. The minute there was trouble, send for Suzy Green. 'We Greens has got a reputation to maintain,' she used to say. And we do, being the richest family on that part of the shore. I suppose she could afford the time as well. There always was two girls to do the work, and one's a pretty good cook. But I never liked it. I wanted her home. Used to think she'd catch her death, travelling God knows how far away, staying in some unheated house looking after the sick, the dying.

"That wasn't the way it happened though. One spring, a man came in a boat to take her round the headland over to the next bay. A woman had died in childbirth. Five children and her husband away in the lumberwoods. No one knew what to do until they could get word to him.

"There wasn't any ice on the water when they set out. But the wind shifted round, like it does. They said after, the boat was trapped in the ice and carried out to sea. The ice never came in again that spring. They found nothing. No splinter of wood. Not a trace."

Ev shuddered. Pansy's story was a bit like her own. After a long moment, she said, "Pansy, can I ask you something?"

"I wouldn't be sitting here on the bathroom floor if I didn't want to talk to you," Pansy said. She smiled, though.

"How long?" Ev paused. This wasn't easy. "How long did it take before you knew she really was dead? Before you could accept it, I mean."

Pansy looked surprised. "Why, even before they got up the search, as soon as we knew what happened, we didn't hold much hope. The sea is some cruel. You know that E.J. Pratt poem they made us learn last year? 'Erosion'? Just like that."

Pansy straightened her spine against the concrete wall

and, looking more solemn than Ev had ever seen her, recited the poem.

"It took the sea a thousand years,
A thousand years to trace
The granite feature of this cliff
In crag and scarp and base.

It took the sea an hour one night,
An hour of storm to place
The sculpture of these granite seams
Upon a woman's face."

"I loves that poem," Pansy said. " 'cause that's exactly what I felt like when they came and told us—like I'd been turned to stone."

Ev remembered how she'd felt when the telegram came. She looked at Pansy in amazement. "Me too," she said.

Pansy smiled as she stood up and offered Ev her hand. "Come on. We'll be in for it if we stays in here forever," she said. "Get your face washed and let's get back before someone comes looking for us."

Ev went to the sink and ran cold water. There were red blotches around her eyes. She looked awful. She bent her head and splashed cool water against her face. The rough paper towel rasped her tender skin. She looked in the mirror again. Not much better.

"You never have given up on your dad, have you?" Pansy asked. There was genuine sympathy in her voice. Ev didn't find that hard to take now.

"No, I never have. Can you keep a secret?"

Pansy nodded.

"I...I wrote to him, every month. I sent letters with his name on them in care of the Red Cross, like you would write to a prisoner of war. I kept hoping one would reach him."

"What happened?"

Ev sighed. "Oh, they came back. Every one of them."

Pansy clucked like a mother hen as she opened the bathroom door. "You poor creature. That's a sin. Now let's get out of here."

When they returned to class, Ev found someone had placed the fallen books neatly on her desk. She had been gone for almost forty-five minutes, but Miss Gould said nothing.

Ev spent the rest of the day in a numbed peace that came from having cried out all her tears. The other girls pretended not to notice her blotchy face as it gradually returned to normal. The pain she felt for her father was still very real, but beneath it was something else—the feeling she'd made a friend.

Chapter Four

The Garden

Ev's chores were finished early Saturday afternoon. She sat on the couch by the front window, her chemistry text open in her lap, waiting for Peter to come to study. By now, all of St. John's was gripped by a strange anticipation. It was a little like waiting for Christmas, without knowing when Christmas would arrive. The Germans had to surrender soon. Everyone knew they were defeated. But they hadn't surrendered yet, and there wouldn't be a V-E Day or any celebration until they did.

V-E Day. After waiting so long for the war to be over, for victory to finally arrive, it was either easy to wait another day or two, or impossibly hard. Or both. Ev couldn't decide. Maybe it was this waiting that made it so difficult to sit still. She realized that she had been staring at the periodic table of elements for at least fifteen minutes without seeing a thing. This is no good, she thought, snapping the book shut. Ian was napping. Annie would be here when he woke up. Ev grabbed her coat in the hall. It was drizzling outside. She could walk by the harbour, maybe see Peter's boat on its way over.

But as soon as Ev stepped out the door, an aimlessness overtook her. Her ambition to walk along the harbour dissolved in the light drizzle that enfolded her. The clouds could not be thick though, because the foggy air was bright.

The slushy winter had given way to a long, grey spring. Ev gathered that spring was a warm, colourful season in other parts of the world, but here in Newfoundland it was mostly cheerless, cold and foggy. And it could easily drag on until the end of June. Here it is May, Ev thought, and the crocuses aren't even out. Most years, the daffodils are up by now.

She wandered to the back of the Thorne house where the grassy lawn gave way to the rising slope of the massive South Side Hills. Someone had made a garden here. Even the incline was carefully terraced and covered in flower beds set at whatever angle the terrain allowed. There were some wooden benches and even a stone pedestal, now empty. Ev wondered what it was for. A path curved up the slope among the flower beds, with stone steps where the hill was steep.

This was the view from Ev's bedroom. Over the past few months, she had watched the garden emerge from the snow with growing interest. It was all so carefully planned, and apparently still cared for. Just last fall, spruce boughs had been placed over the beds to protect the plants for winter. Were they okay now? She walked up to the nearest flower bed and raised a bough. In the sodden puddles of rotting leaves that were last year's perennials, a few tender green fronds tentatively unfurled. Among those plants, dozens of spring bulbs poked up knifelike shoots, seeking a sun that seldom showed itself. They were pale but strong looking. Ev had to smile. This is where you find spring in Newfoundland, she thought. Not up in the sky, but here in the ground.

"Are you interested in gardening?"

The voice behind her was gentle, but so near and unexpected that Ev gasped, dropped the bough and whirled around.

"I'm sorry, Evelyn. I didn't mean to startle you." John Thorne turned bright red and looked at the ground. "Actually, I came around to take these boughs off. It's time now. Any longer and the plants will grow deformed." Ev noticed he was dressed in even older clothes than usual. Work clothes. They didn't suit him. He still looked scholarly, professional, his fingernails perfectly clean.

Ev would have bolted, but John Thorne didn't give her a chance. "See how the daffodils are coming?" he asked, raising the bough Ev had dropped and moving it aside. "And these," he pointed to some wrinkled, almost grey leaves. "They don't look like much now, but just watch. One day next week, you'll look out and they'll be blooming all over the garden."

So he was the gardener. Ev found herself looking where he pointed.

"You take Latin, don't you?" he asked.

Ev nodded in spite of herself. Latin was one of her favourite subjects.

He pointed to the wrinkled little plant again. "*Pulmonaria officinalis*. That's the Latin name. What does that suggest to you?"

"Something to do with lungs?"

"Right! Here, look at this." He picked one of the tiny new leaves and handed it to Ev. It was lobe-shaped and looked as if it was splashed with silver paint. "See how it looks like a lung?" He caught her sceptical look. "No, you're right, it doesn't look exactly like a lung, but you have to imagine yourself back in the Middle Ages. Maybe you've never seen a real lung—"

"Which I haven't," Ev said, but she couldn't disguise her interest now.

"—or even a picture of a lung because books are rare. But you've been told that there's a divine plan. That the plants that can cure certain organs *look* like the organs they can cure. Then this leaf might look like a lung. *Pulmonaria officinalis*. The common name is lungwort. *Officinalis* indicates medicinal use. All of which tell us that this humble garden flower had a former life as a respected medicine, used to treat respiratory ailments. And the idea I just described, that the cure would resemble the organ, was called the doctrine of signatures." It was the longest John Thorne had ever spoken to Ev. He must have realized this, because he suddenly turned away to remove the rest of the boughs, as if taken aback by his own boldness.

Ev realized he had no intention of continuing. Just when he had her attention. She came to the bed where he was working and started removing boughs with him. "Did it work?" she asked.

"Did what work?"

"The doctrine of signatures."

John Thorne paused, a bough held in mid-air like an exotic fan. "Good Lord, no. It was an idea born of desperation. Like most medicine, in fact, until very recently. People dying like flies of every kind of disease imaginable. Why? They had no idea. Miasma. Know what that is?"

"No."

"Bad air. People used to think illnesses were caused by bad air. Anyone ever tell you night air is unhealthy?"

Ev nodded.

"Miasma."

"What a load of miasma," Ev said.

John Thorne smiled. "Let's do this bed over here now,"

he said. Then he continued, "No, not really. It was based on sound observation. Things that smell bad, food and water for example, tend to make you sick. People had no way of knowing bacteria made the smell. All sorts of ideas like that persist even now, centuries after the discovery of bacteria. Look!" he interrupted himself. "Even the hyacinths are coming through. A few days of sunny weather and this place will be transformed."

They worked in silence.

"Why is a cold a cold?" John Thorne said after a moment.

Ev laughed. "Is this a joke, like, when is a door not a door?"

"No," he said, but he laughed too. "A cold is called a cold because people used to think the illness was caused by coldness entering the body. Literally. Which is why your mother makes sure you're warmly dressed in the winter."

There was a pause. Ev wished he hadn't mentioned her mother. She had been enjoying herself.

But Doctor Thorne didn't notice. "That's why people still believe newborn babies should be kept in stiflingly hot rooms," he continued. "And women were supposed to stay bundled up in bed for nine days after giving birth in case they caught cold—meaning an infection following childbirth in that case."

"Sure, Nan could tell you all about that." Peter's voice came from behind them.

"Yes, indeed, Peter," John Thorne said as he turned. "I've talked to her about it many times."

Ev watched Peter take the situation in. His face registered surprise and amusement, maybe even a faint hint of I-told-you-so. Ev wished he hadn't caught her like this. She had actually enjoyed being with John Thorne. Now, she made herself frown again.

"Come on, Peter," she said, and she left the yard without another word. Whatever that feeling had been, it was wrong. She would never let herself feel that way again.

Peter didn't speak until they were inside the house. "You didn't have to be so rude to him," he said.

Ev took off her coat and hung it up, slipped out of her shoes, walked into the sitting room and sat down in the wingback chair. What could she say? She had just betrayed her father. To have done such a thing was bad enough. How could she admit it? She couldn't. She couldn't have explained herself to anyone except—Pansy Green. They hadn't really talked since Thursday, but Ev suddenly realized she would rather talk to Pansy about how she felt than Peter. And she'd always told Peter everything.

Ev looked down at her hands. They were dirty from the garden. She stood up. "I have to wash my hands," she said. I have to be alone for a minute, she thought. She bolted from the room and up the stairs. In the bathroom, she scrubbed her hands harder than she needed to. Why can't my feelings stay the way I want them to? she thought. Then she could hate Doctor Thorne forever, and Peter would always be her best friend. Why don't feelings just stay put? She dried her hands angrily and took a deep breath.

As Ev turned to the stairs, a thin, tuneless fragment of song floated out into the hall.

"...working on the railroad, all the ding dong day..."

She poked Ian's door open. He was lying on his back, singing, while he flew Melodus over his head in time to the music. "Ian," she said, "it's 'live long day,' not 'ding dong day.'" She walked over and ruffled his hair. "Are you awake?"

As she watched, the light of mischief came into Ian's dark blue eyes. "Not yet," he said.

"Yet," Ev said. "Yet." It was their joke from when Ian was just learning to talk.

Ian giggled. "Not yet." Then he changed his mind. "Give Ian an up."

Ev caught him up in her arms. "Ian, you monkey. Let's go see Peter."

"Melodus too," Ian said, reaching down for the bird.

Ev carried him downstairs. Here, at least, was the one person she would always feel exactly the same about, would always love perfectly, just as she did now.

When Peter saw Ian, he smiled. "Ian," Peter said. "Just the lad to help us with the periodic table of elements."

Ev dumped Ian onto the couch beside Peter and sat Melodus on a nearby table.

Peter picked up his chemistry book. "Once upon a time," he said, "there were six noble gases and their names were?" He looked at Ev.

"Um, helium, neon, argon,"

"He's the one in Shakespeare," Peter interrupted.

"In Shakespeare?"

"Yes, maid. In *Merchant of Venice*. Remember?

Ev shook her head. "I don't recall any noble gases in that play."

"Sure, the Duke of Argon. He wants to marry Portia in the first act."

"I think that's the Duke of Aragon."

"They weren't particular about spelling back then," Peter said.

"Okay. The Duke of Argon, the Earl of Krypton,"

"Now, he's the one knows Superman," Peter said to Ian.

"Peter! That's not fair."

"You're right. This is my story." He looked at Ian again. "And Lord Xenon and the Earl of Radon. Six noble gases. What was it about these gases that made them so noble, you ask? That's a very good question, Ian my son. Most gases are not noble. Take methane for example. When diapers are changed, are those noble gases we smell?"

Ian held his nose and giggled.

"Right you are, my son."

Ev jumped in. "The gases were called noble because they kept themselves apart from all the other elements," she said.

"That's right, Ian. These gases were snobs. Did they mix freely, creating compounds as they went, like other elements?"

Ian shook his head.

"Some clever you are," Peter said. "Two and a half and you knows your high school chemistry. No, they did not. These noble gases were— " he looked at Ev again.

"Inert."

"Inert it is. And can we think of another inert element with noble connotations?"

"Gold," Ev said.

"Gold indeed. Give that girl a gold star."

Ian giggled.

That was the chemistry lesson—Peter and Ev laughing their way through the periodic table. Ev knew their classmates thought of them as drudges, spending hours poring over their books. If they could see the fun we have, she thought, wouldn't they be surprised. Of course, it only worked if you knew most of the answers to begin with, so there was a fair bit of poring over books alone, but the work was worth the fun they had studying together. The moment of strangeness between Peter and Ev was gone.

When they finished the noble gases, Ian lost interest in chemistry and decided Melodus should host a tea party for all the other stuffed birds. He collected his china doll dishes, a puffin, a pigeon (which *Native Birds and Mammals of North America* called the European rock dove), a common murre and an eider (which was too heavy for him to manage alone and interrupted the alkaline earth metals). While they studied, Ev watched the tea party from the corner of her eye. It was all very civilized until the puffin insulted the European rock dove by calling him a pigeon.

"Pigeon, pigeon, pigeon," taunted the puffin in a high voice, waggling in a most provoking manner.

"Not pigeon," cried the European rock dove, and he kicked the china doll dishes in all directions, scattering the bird food, which Ian had painstakingly made by tearing up pieces of newspaper, all over the living room. Then the eider got out a machine gun and shot all the other birds (and himself) to pieces. Ev's mother arrived home, loaded down with packages, just as the dead birds settled comfortably among the scattered china and little bits of paper.

"Oh dear," she said. "What happened here?"

Ian smiled like an angel. "Birds have tea party," he said.

"Sorry, Mum." Ev scrambled to the floor. "Time for the birds to tidy up, Ian."

Ian shook his head. "Birds all dead now."

41

Peter picked up the eider. "Look, Ian," he said in a quacking voice. "I'm alive."

Ian giggled.

"Peter, could you get Ian to help you tidy this mess while I deal with these parcels? He has to learn to pick up after himself."

Peter nodded.

"Thank you, dear. Ian, when I come back up here, I want the room to look just the way it did before I went out. Do you understand?"

"Yes, Mummy."

"Good." Ev's mother handed half her parcels to Ev. "Here. Come and help me put these away, please."

Ev followed her mother downstairs to the kitchen. The serious note in her voice led Ev to expect a lecture about letting Ian run wild. She tried to intercept.

"I should have been paying more attention to the mess Ian was making," she began. "Peter and I were studying."

"Well, it was a mess, but I'm sure there's no damage done."

So that wasn't it. What then?

Annie sat in the kitchen, reading the Saturday paper.

"Annie," Ev's mother said as she dumped her packages on the table, "Ian's scattered bits of paper all over the front room. Could you check and see if they're picked up now? You might need the vacuum cleaner." Ev wondered if her mother was just trying to get Annie out of the room so they could talk.

Annie sighed loudly, but did as she was told. As she disappeared up the stairs, Ev's mother turned to her.

"I ran into Doctor Thorne. He was leaving the garden as I was coming in just now," she said.

So that was it. He must have told her I was rude to him, Ev thought. She busied herself with the contents of the brown paper bags, waiting for the lecture.

"He said you had quite a nice chat in the garden."

"He did?" Ev almost dropped a package of tea.

Ev's mother look puzzled. "Yes. You did talk to him, didn't you?"

Ev nodded.

"That's good. Ev, Doctor Thorne has been very kind to us. The war made it almost impossible to find a place to rent. He could easily get twice, even three times as much rent as we're paying. If not for him, we'd still be living with your grandparents. And your grandmother and I have tried, but I don't think I could have lived with her much longer and maintained my sanity."

Ev smiled. That was true.

Her mother continued. "He's a very kind man, Ev, and lonely. I don't think he eats well in that boardinghouse, and it's more or less our fault he's there. When I was talking to him, it struck me that I could at least repay him with a decent meal. He's coming for dinner tomorrow."

Ev picked up a brown paper bag and folded it into a neat, thick rectangle. She pictured Sunday dinner. Her family around the table, John Thorne sitting where her father ought to be. She looked at her mother steadily. "Are you in love with him?"

Her mother's face drained of colour. "Oh, Evelyn. How can you think such a thing?"

So she wasn't. "I just...it's just..." Ev's voice trailed into a whisper. "It's what people are saying. About you and him." She ought to know.

"Who says?" Her mother's voice was suddenly very quiet. "Everyone." Ev rushed on. "Girls at school, and they hear it from their mothers. Peter knows. Some women even spoke to Mrs. Bursey."

Ev's mother sat down. She put a hand to her forehead. "People have no right. I'm just doing the best I can for my family. How can they be so unkind?" Her voice was filled with disbelief and despair.

Ev wished she'd never spoken. "I'm sorry, Mummy, I didn't mean to—" But she stopped because that was a lie. She had meant to.

Her mother smiled weakly. "It's all right, Evelyn." She rose from her chair and tidied away the last of the packages. "If that's what people think." She paused, then continued as if something had just fallen into place. "If that's what John Thorne thinks, we'll just have to show them, won't we?" There was a strange glint in her mother's eye. "We won't be having anyone to supper tomorrow after all. Why don't you go see how Peter and Ian are making out upstairs."

Ev nodded. The kitchen she left behind was perfectly tidy, but she could not shake the feeling she was walking away from some kind of wreckage.

That night, Ev came into the hall, closing Ian's door gently. She had given him a bath, read *Millions of Cats*, kissed him, tucked him in and kissed Melodus too. Her mother's voice carried up from below. The only phone was in the downstairs hall. It was impossible to have a private phone conversation in this house.

"Yes, well, I'm sorry. I completely forgot we'd been invited out for supper." She didn't sound sorry. "No, not Ev's grandparents. People you wouldn't know." Ev almost groaned out loud. In this city, the doctors knew everyone. Her mother was such a bad liar. "I really must go." *Click.* She hadn't even said goodbye. Ev waited for her mother to get up so she could creep to her own room without being discovered. There was complete silence in the hall below, then a sniff, then a sob. Ev bolted for her room and closed the door as quietly as she could.

Before she went to bed, Ev turned out the light and stood by her window, looking at the garden. It was going to be beautiful. And she would have to look at it all summer. Doctor Thorne could have told her mother how rude she'd been. Most adults would.

"*Pulmonaria officinalis,*" she said softly under her breath. It was a nice scrap of information. Daddy would have liked it. What I did today was for him, Ev thought. If that's true, why do I feel so miserable?

Shut up, she told herself as she climbed into bed.

Chapter Five

To the Battery

On Tuesday morning, Ev woke with the sun in her face. The sky outside her window was a clear china blue, untouched by even a feather of a cloud.

V-E Day, finally. Even the weather was celebrating. They hadn't seen the sun for so long, Ev couldn't remember when at first. Then she did. That day last week when the soldier stared at her from across the river. At least he seems to be gone, she thought. Peter worries too much.

Ev smiled as she got dressed. No school, and Peter would be here soon. But it wasn't a holiday at the hospital. Ev stole a guilty glance at her alarm clock. After ten. Her mother would be long gone. She sighed her relief. Since Saturday, her mother was different. She went to bed early, hardly ate at all. It seemed like an effort for her even to play with Ian. Ev tried not to think why.

Ian. Where was that monkey? He would sneak into her room to wake her up when he could. Not today. Their mother must have told him not to. Ev dressed as quickly as she could and went downstairs.

The kitchen was big and not too gloomy for a basement. Some high windows at the back let the daylight in. Annie was washing the breakfast dishes. Ian sat on the floor near the table. He had made a village out of unpainted wooden blocks.

His wooden truck was parked beside a house. He was carefully moving his one metal truck, a precious red fire engine, between wooden block houses. Melodus was driving while Ian made siren noises.

Ev squatted beside him. "Where's the fire, Ian?"

Ian pointed to a house. It was knocked over. "Put fire out now. Then Grandpa and Doctor T'orn fix people."

The smile faded from Ev's face. Luckily, Ian was too busy with his fire to notice. She sat at the table and poured herself a bowl of cereal. Ian's attachment to Doctor Thorne was strong. Convincing her mother to stop seeing him was almost too easy, like an accident. Ev realized that Ian wasn't likely to give Doctor Thorne up so quickly. If she wanted that to happen, she'd have to make it happen. The idea made her feel sick. But then she looked at Ian, playing at her feet. He'll never know his father, Ev thought. Why should I feel bad about trying to keep things the way they are? She didn't let herself answer that question.

After breakfast, Ev knelt on the floor beside Ian. "Let's tidy up now, kiddo. Peter's coming." Together, they put the blocks away. It was important to behave now, to make things easier for Mum.

Peter arrived just as Ev brought Ian upstairs.

"Well, my son," he said, "what about that boat ride you've been wanting?"

Ian clapped his hands.

"I thought so," Peter said to Ev. "Nan'd like to see you both today if that's okay."

Ev nodded. She missed Mrs. Bursey now that they lived so far away. "Just let me tell Annie Ian's coming with us," she said.

When they stepped outside, a soft breeze ruffled Ev's hair. In the long, grey spring, it was easy to forget that a wind could be something other than a stinging slap. She breathed deeply. The air smelled of living things. A cluster of crocuses had opened by the front steps, purple and yellow in the sun. Yesterday, they were nothing more than spears of green.

"Walk between Peter and me," Ev told Ian. "Hold our hands. That way, you'll be safe if there's traffic." Ian did as he was told. They didn't talk as they walked along South Side Road. They didn't need to.

The sharp smell of coal reached Ev's nose before she saw the Dawe premises. Coal dust permeated the ground in this place. The fenced yards around the Dawe warehouse were usually full of coal, huge black hills of it, unloaded from boats, waiting for the fleet of Dawe trucks. Not now. Three trucks sat idle in front of the office and the yard was almost empty. This spring, there was barely enough coal to go around.

Peter followed Ev's gaze. "They say new shipments are on the way from Nova Scotia now," he said. "Coal and salt." He smiled. "We'll soon be throwing those ration books away. No more shortages."

When they reached the *Evelyn's Pride*, Ev carefully handed Ian down to Peter. That one moment when Ian hovered over the dangerous slice of water between the wharf and the boat always chilled her. She would have liked a life jacket for Ian, but there weren't any small enough to fit him. Ev climbed down and Peter gave Ian back to her. She held him in her lap, warm and small, her perfect brother on this perfect day. She didn't cuddle him, though. Ian didn't mind being held, but he only cuddled when he wanted to.

Peter started the engine and the boat eased out into the

harbour. From the shadows of the buildings that hugged the waterfront, they sailed into the full sunlight of this lovely day. Across the harbour, the wooden houses of St. John's ranged up the hills, bright in the sun. It was as if the world had changed overnight from a black and white photograph into colour.

Then, somewhere in the city, a church bell rang. Ev heard car horns and more church bells. Ships' bells and whistles joined the growing din. Peter cut the boat's engine and they drifted for a moment. Under everything, Ev heard people laughing and shouting. The harbour filled with sounds that echoed off the water and the high rock hills until the whole city resonated with a joyful noise. She glanced at her watch. Noon. The war was over. Peter whooped and threw his cap into the air, but carefully, so it landed in the boat. Ev hugged Ian closer. He'd stiffened a little when the noise began, but laughed when he saw their smiles.

The last echo finally died. The cries of a few gulls, the ruffle of a breeze and the slap of water against the hull were the only sounds. Peter smiled at Ev. For the first time in six long years, they listened to the silence of peace. She turned Ian in her lap so she could see him. "The war is over, Ian. Now, everything will be good again." She hoped that speaking the words might make them true. After a long moment, Peter started the engine again. They crossed the Narrows to the Battery.

The waterfront on the South Side was lined with businesses, but the Battery was different. Here, only houses and fishing stores perched against a rock face that rose steeply, bare of trees and hardly touched by grass. The Battery sat close to the open sea. It was the least sheltered part of the harbour, but the view was magnificent.

Mrs. Bursey hugged Ev as she came into the small house. "Oh, my dear, you're after getting some tall," she said. It was true. Every time Ev saw her, Peter's grandmother seemed smaller and frailer. Now she looked as if she might blow away in a puff of wind.

Ev looked around the small house. Everything was old and a bit shabby, but perfectly neat and clean, just as it had been when she first came here in the fall of 1942. In that dark and confusing time, when the outcome of the war was so uncertain and Ev's life was in flux, this had always been a place of refuge.

Dinner was waiting for them—chicken soup. Ian didn't like soup, so Peter got him some bread and cheese. When they were finished, Ev helped clear the table. "I'll give you a hand with the dishes if you like," she offered.

"That'd be lovely, child," Mrs. Bursey said. Peter's grandmother called everyone child. Ev didn't mind.

"Perhaps I'll take Ian on a bit of an excursion," Peter said.

"Excursion? But you won't take him far, will you?"

Peter smiled as if to reassure her. "Just up the path to the lookout, Ev. I'll hold his hand every step of the way."

When they turned around, Ian was already holding Peter's cane out to him. Everyone laughed.

Like many houses in the Battery, this one had no running water. Ev fetched a kettle of water for the dishes from a pail by the door.

"No sense in starting till the water's heated," Mrs. Bursey said, setting the kettle on the stove. She smiled at Ev. "Well, Evelyn, I didn't know I'd live to see this day. Times it seemed as if the war would last forever. And now our lives will all get back to normal."

Ev nodded. That was just what she wanted too.

"Peter tells me it's you and him competing for this scholarship."

"And Stan Dawe," Ev said. She pretended to study the tablecloth when she said his name, hoping Mrs. Bursey wouldn't look at her.

"What do the Dawes be needing with a scholarship?" Mrs. Bursey snorted. "Richest coal merchants on the island."

"They can't be making much these days, though. We saw the yards this morning. They're empty."

"Well, that'll right itself now. So you've decided to be an engineer, have you?"

Ev nodded, but then she shook her head. "Maybe. I'm not sure. I'd like to do it for my father's sake, you know? But the truth is, I don't really know what I want to be. Nothing's really grabbed me yet. Do you understand?"

"I do indeed. I was only about your age when I found myself alone with a neighbour woman, about to give birth. Her husband gone for the granny. That's what we used to call the midwife, you see? Back in a minute, he said, just keep your eye on things. Height of the fishing season. Every woman and child busy spreading fish on the flakes to dry, most of the men gone in the boats.

"Well, the granny was looking after some woman cut her hand with a splitting knife. Bad cut. Had to be sewed. Must have been close to an hour before she could come. They found us in that woman's bedroom, me, the lady and her baby, already cleaned and dressed, asleep in her mother's arms. That old midwife looked at me and she said, 'I guess you belongs to me now, my dear. You got the nerve for this job.' She laughed, but I knew it was true. Started going round with her after that, been at it ever since. When your life's work comes looking for you, you'll know it right enough."

Was that true? Ev wondered. She'd never felt anything like that.

"And how is your mother these days, my dear?" Mrs. Bursey asked.

Ev knew this was a perfectly innocent question. Mrs. Bursey had cared for Ev's mother when she was pregnant with Ian. In those terrible days after the telegram came, Mrs. Bursey was the one who helped Ev's mother most. It should have been an easy question. But it wasn't.

"Well, she seems to be getting along with her upgrading," Ev said, opting for the easiest answer.

Mrs. Bursey nodded. "Your grandfather told me she'll have her nursing qualifications up to date in just a few months. And I imagine the new house is doing her some good?"

Ev knew this was as close as Mrs. Bursey ever came to probing. She also knew she could talk more honestly to Mrs. Bursey than any other adult.

"Oh, Mrs. Bursey, I don't know if we should have moved in there at all. It's been good for Mum, I know it has, but the gossip is terrible."

"There's always some got no better to do than mind other people's business, child. There always will be. You can't let people like that govern your life." Mrs. Bursey poured out the hot water and began to wash the dishes.

"But, it's not as if they're lying."

"Why child, whatever do you mean?"

Ev felt herself grow hot with shame, but she continued. "If you saw the way Doctor Thorne looks whenever Mum's name is mentioned." She stabbed a dish angrily with the tea towel. Mrs. Bursey knew Doctor Thorne. Ev waited for a lecture on his virtues.

"And how do you think your mother feels?"

This wasn't what Ev expected. How did her mother feel? "Well, I don't even think she knew people were talking." Ev stopped. This was more than she'd wanted to say.

Mrs. Bursey said nothing. For a while, they did the dishes together in silence. Ev knew, if she chose to, she could change the subject and it would not be raised again. But she needed to talk. When she spoke, her voice was barely a whisper. "I told her," she said. "I told her what people are saying. I had to."

"And how did she take it, child?" There was no hint of anger in Mrs. Bursey's voice, only concern.

"Remember what she used to be like, when you first met her? She's a bit like that again." It was hard to remember those days when Ev's mother had done nothing but sleep and cry. Ev didn't want her to be like that now. She waited for Mrs. Bursey to tell her that her mother had a right to go on with her life, that it wasn't Ev's place to interfere. All the things Ev knew. But Mrs. Bursey said nothing at first. She washed the rest of the dishes before she spoke again.

"Sit with me a while," she said finally, and they sat together at the table. "The war ends today, Evelyn. It's behind us now. But people were called upon to make sacrifices that should never be asked, and you were one of them. Such a heavy weight was placed on your shoulders, my child. You've done well, though, and your mother too. I'm going to speak plainly to you, Evelyn. You're old enough now. Your mother is trying to get her life in order. She still loves your father very much. But you can't expect her to close the door on life forever. She's far too young for that.

"As for Doctor Thorne, when his mother was alive, that man had no scrap of a life to call his own. Now, for the first time, he's free to do what he wants. Does he drink and gamble and run around with women?" Mrs. Bursey smiled. "No, he gives his house over to a young woman with children and moves into a boardinghouse. He's a fine doctor and a good man." She paused. "But the heart has a mind of its own. He can't help what he feels for your mother. Even if she's not of the same mind." She patted Ev's hand again and rose.

Ev thought for a moment, then spoke. "You know what you just said, about the heart having a mind of its own?"

Mrs. Bursey nodded.

"Well, my heart has a mind of its own too. When I was little, I always felt exactly what I wanted to feel. Now, what I feel isn't the same as what I want to feel."

Mrs. Bursey nodded. "You're growing up."

"But my heart is still with my father. And I don't ever want that to change. It's almost as if, well, he'll still be alive as long as he stays in my heart. And Ian will never know him. I'm the only one."

"It's perfectly natural to feel that way, Evelyn."

Ev took a deep breath and went on. This wasn't easy to talk about. "But then, if I'm the one who has to keep him in my heart, how can I do anything else? It's as if everything inside me has to stay frozen."

Mrs. Bursey smiled. "You grow bigger, child, and you can do things you never did before. The heart grows too. In time, you may find there's room for other people. And your father will still have his place as well." Mrs. Bursey sighed. "You're a strong person, Ev."

Ev smiled. "My father always told me that."

"It's true. Stronger than your mother, I think. But there's a danger, sometimes, in strength. It means you can get what you want if you try, but getting what you want isn't always the best thing."

Ev wanted to ask Mrs. Bursey what she meant, but just then the door flew open and Ian rushed in, flinging himself at Ev. "We saw bald eagle!" he cried.

"Really?"

Peter nodded. "A pair. Must've been looking for nesting birds in the cliffs."

Ian yawned.

"Time for your nap, Ian," Ev said.

"Then we'd better get him home."

Ev turned and hugged Mrs. Bursey. It wouldn't be possible to finish that talk now. "Thank you."

"Any time you need a chat, my dear, you knows I'm here."

Chapter Six

Getting Ian Home

Ian was sound asleep in Ev's lap before they were halfway across the harbour. When Peter cut the engine at the Dawe wharf, Ev knew she had a problem. "Ian's too heavy for me to carry," she said. "I'm not sure what to do."

"Perhaps I could take the boat under the bridge."

Ev frowned. "Even if you could, I'd never get up the bank with him. It's too steep there. But don't worry, I'll be okay." She knew Peter could not handle both Ian and his cane.

With Peter's help, Ev slung Ian over her shoulder. He felt like a rag doll stuffed with wet sawdust. Scrambling up the wooden ladder was hard work. By the time Ev stood on the wharf, her arms were already shaky.

Peter gazed up at her from the boat. "I can't see how you're going to manage."

"Having trouble?"

Ev turned to find herself face to face with Stan Dawe. "Not really," she said. She shifted Ian awkwardly and tried to look nonchalant, as if walking around with a sleeping, thirty-five-pound two-year-old on her shoulder was the most natural thing in the world. Her daydreams of chance meetings with Stan were nothing like this.

"Evelyn needs help getting her brother home," Peter said from his boat. "I'm not much good at carrying things. Perhaps you'd give her a hand." It was the sensible thing to say. Trust Peter to be sensible.

Stan smiled. "Always happy to help a lady."

Ev could hardly believe this was happening. To hide her embarrassment, she leaned over, as best she could, to talk to Peter. "Why don't you come by later on? I think Mum might be glad of a little company."

Peter nodded, started the boat's engine and waved goodbye.

Ev turned to face Stan Dawe again. There was an awkward pause. "I could drive," he suggested.

"You have your licence?" Ev couldn't recall seeing Stan drive. The girls at school would surely have made enough fuss for anyone to remember.

"Well, almost."

Ev shook her head. Ian wasn't getting into any car with an unlicenced driver, no matter how short the drive.

"Well, then, you'd better give him over," Stan said. Ev blushed. How to hand Ian over without Stan touching her? She wasn't strong enough to simply thrust her brother out in front of her. Stan took a step towards her and Ev, without thinking, stepped back.

"Watch out!" Stan cried.

Ev looked behind her. She was standing at the very edge of the wharf. This was ridiculous. "I'm sorry. It's just...I'm just...here." She stepped forward and allowed him to remove Ian from her arms. In the process, the back of Stan's hand brushed her breast. It wasn't as if he meant to. It was unavoidable. He didn't look at her, but that wasn't much help. If not for Ian, Ev might well have turned around and walked off the edge of the wharf to escape her mortification.

"You live above the bridge, right?" Stan asked. Some of the brashness was gone from his tone. He seemed embarrassed too. Ev liked him for that.

"Yes. You know where the old Thorne house is?"

Stan nodded. "I help with deliveries sometimes. Dad wants me to learn the business 'from the cellar up.' His little joke," Stan said. But he didn't smile.

Ian looked very light in Stan's strong arms. During the awkward transfer, he'd barely stirred. Ev had to admit there was something about Stan that left her slightly weak in the knees. She had to force herself to think of something intelligent to say. Ev remembered her conversation with Mrs. Bursey about the scholarship. "If you're supposed to take over here " — she nodded at the warehouse and office as they passed— "what's the scholarship for?"

Stan snorted. "The future. You think people are going to heat with coal forever?" He didn't wait for Ev's reply. "I want to study chemical engineering." He kicked a stray fragment of coal on the road. "I don't know if this black stuff has a future, but I know where to find out—in a lab. Dad doesn't see it. Expects me to start working here as soon as I graduate. But I figure, if I get the scholarship, he'll have to let me go."

"Oh," Ev said. It made sense now. She had imagined someone like Stan would be able to do anything he wanted.

"What about you? What kind of engineering would you study?"

A hard question. The fact was, Ev hardly ever thought about engineering. "Well, my father was a civil engineer, so I guess that's what I'd do. He supervised the building of hydro dams. That's why we always lived outside St. John's, until the war." Somehow, it seemed natural to talk about her father on this day. "And then, when the war came, he thought he'd be useful, because he knew about explosives. He worked with them all the time." Suddenly, Ev hated engineering. If her father had done something else with his life, he might still be alive.

Stan must have noticed the frown on her face. "You don't know what happened to him, do you?" he said.

Ev sighed. "No. I guess now we never will."

"I suppose not. That must be tough. Especially now with everyone coming home." He paused. "You know, there's a train full of troops coming into the station tonight, home from the war."

"How could that be? The war just ended." The news left Ev slightly dazed.

"Yeah, it's a coincidence. They were coming home on leave, but now I guess they can stay. Some of them haven't been home since they first went overseas."

Ev was still trying to get her mind around this idea. "How do you know?"

"Everyone knows. It's in today's paper. One of them is our neighbour's nephew. People got telegrams. They know who's coming and all."

Ev said nothing. It seemed incredibly unkind of Stan to tell her this today. She'd learned a lot about unkindness from girls like Letty Winsor at school. Was this deliberate? She glanced at Stan. If he meant to be unkind, he'd watch for her reaction. But he carried Ian without glancing at her. He wasn't cruel, Ev realized. He had no idea how this news hurt her.

They passed St. Mary's, the stone church near the bridge.

So here I am, Ev thought, with the most popular boy in the school. Her heart raced just because he walked beside her.

Ian murmured in his sleep. "Oh no," Ev said, "I hope he doesn't wake up. He should have a longer nap."

Stan nodded towards the bundle slumped in his arms. "He means a lot to you, doesn't he?"

"Yes. Yes, he does. He was born just after we found out about Dad. He does mean a lot to me." Ev knew she was repeating herself. She couldn't help it. The words to explain what Ian meant to her hadn't been invented.

"It's funny," Stan said. "I didn't think you were the type."

"What type?"

"The type to go crazy over a little kid. I thought you were all books and studying."

"Well, Ian isn't just any little kid," Ev said. "He likes a lot of things I like."

Stan eyed her suspiciously, as if he thought she was joking. "Like what?"

Ev told him about *Native Birds and Mammals of North America*, about the stuffed animals in the Thorne house and Melodus.

"Oh yeah?" Stan said when she finished. "Maybe I should meet this kid when he's awake."

Was he saying he wanted to see her again? "He's more fun when he's awake," she said. "Lighter too."

They reached the Thorne house. "Could you bring him inside?" Ev asked.

"Sure."

When Ev opened the front door, sunlight flooded in after them. Her mother stood in the hall, holding a tea tray. "I was afraid he'd fall asleep," she said when she saw Ian.

"Like clockwork. Mum, this is Stan Dawe from Prince of Wales. He was by the wharf when Peter brought us home."

"Well, thank you, Stan. He's getting too heavy for us to carry." She smiled. "I'm so glad he's home. John wants to take him for a walk later."

John? Ev was still trying to figure out who John was when Doctor Thorne appeared in the living room doorway.

"Hello, Evelyn," he said.

Chapter Seven

Cedar Waxwings

"I'll take the tea tray if you like, Nina." Her mother's name sounded very natural on Doctor Thorne's tongue.

"Oh, thank you, John." Nina McCallum gave him the tray, and Doctor Thorne disappeared into the front room. Stan placed Ian in Ev's mother's arms. "Will you stay for tea Stan?"

"No, thank you, Mrs. McCallum. I've actually got work to do down to the warehouse office."

"Today?" Ev said.

"There won't be time after the coal arrives," Stan said. "And it's finally on its way. There's some trouble with the accounts. Nothing serious, but Dad thought an extra pair of eyes might help so he asked me spend a few hours at it. I'm not in anyone's way because of the holiday."

"Yes, they even let us off a few hours early at the hospital, if you can believe that. Well, I'd better get this boy upstairs." And she was gone.

As long as Ian was there, it had been possible to talk to Stan, but now, Ev scarcely knew where to look. "Well, thank you," she thought to say.

Stan opened the door. "No trouble." He gave her one of those dazzling smiles.

Ev leaned against the door as it snapped shut. You're almost as bad as Violet Harvey, she told herself. But closing that door was like flipping a switch. Once again, Ev had to face her problems. She wondered if Stan Dawe was a gossip. The idea appalled her. He could tell everyone at school that her mother and Doctor Thorne were here alone. But what on earth was Doctor Thorne doing here? After Saturday, Ev knew her mother had avoided him.

Ev heard the clink of a china teacup in the front room. Her first impulse was to run upstairs, to escape this awful situation her mother had put her in. Then she remembered what Mrs. Bursey had said. Maybe things could change and still be okay. She would give it a try.

Doctor Thorne was sitting on the couch with an empty teacup in his hands. When Ev came into the room, he put it down abruptly. Ev wondered how much he knew about the part she had played in her mother's reaction to him over the past few days. The thought filled her with shame. Say something, she thought, say anything. "I didn't see your car," she said.

"I didn't take it today. Such a fine day, I thought I'd walk. Walked your mother home from the hospital." He was babbling. Strange to be able to make an adult feel so nervous. Then Ev noticed a little Union Jack on a stick on the table. Doctor Thorne followed her gaze. "I brought it for Ian," he said. "I would have bought you one too." He paused.

"No. I'm too old for that."

"I thought as much. When Ian wakes up, I'd like to take him for a bit of a walk. If he wants to, of course."

Ev forced herself to be nice. "I'm sure he'd like that," she said. Then she went a little further. "He likes you."

A smile smoothed the creases of worry from Doctor Thorne's face, and a flood of words tumbled out of him. "Everyone's out walking around. Strange holiday, no parades or anything, people just walking around, feeling happy." He was almost pathetic in his gratitude.

"You'll have to excuse me. I've got some schoolwork to do," Ev lied. This is all I can manage for now, she thought.

"Yes, yes, of course," Doctor Thorne said, but she could see his disappointment.

Ev rushed upstairs, passing her mother in the hall. She didn't stop when her mother spoke her name, didn't stop until the door of her room was safely closed behind her. Two hot tears trailed down her cheeks as she pressed her back to the door. Would it always be this hard? she wondered. Would it always feel this strange?

I want my father. The thought formed itself in her head, clear and hard and painful as a lump of glass. I want my father. She slumped, exhausted. Then she went over to her bed, curled up and escaped into sleep.

When Ev woke, the light that filtered through her window told her the day was almost over. She felt peaceful, as if something wonderful had happened. Why? She lay very still, trying to track the feeling back to its source. A sparrow hopped on a branch outside her window.

Birds. She had dreamed about the birds, a long time ago, when she was a little girl. Something she had forgotten.

She had been what? Seven or eight. It was morning in Belbin's Cove, and the light of the first snowfall shone on her ceiling when she opened her eyes.

"Ev, Ev, wake up and get dressed. Come outside, but be very quiet." Her father's voice came up the stairs, full of urgent, happy mystery. Ev dressed and rushed downstairs. Her mother was busy at the stove. Her mother so tall, Ev had to look up at her. "Go see your father," she'd said. "Have breakfast later."

"What is it?" Ev asked. What could be so special?

Her mother laughed, pulled Ev's coat around her and kissed her cheek. "Just go and look, but don't run, and keep quiet."

Ev pulled on her boots and mittens and tip-toed out the back door. Her father stood there, strong and tall, not moving. His breath made a puffy halo around his bare head. He was looking at something hidden by the back of the house. Then he looked at Ev and smiled. "Come here," he whispered. "Come quietly."

It wasn't hard to be quiet. The new snow was as soft as feathers. Ev held her breath until she reached her father. He bent and lifted her effortlessly in a single, strong swoop. "Look," he said.

The dogberry tree behind the house was loaded with bright orange berries. Hanging from the bunches, shaking off the snow, were dozens of little birds. Smooth beige birds. They had little black masks across their faces and peaked feather caps, almost like small blue jays. They weren't raucous like jays, though. They were quiet, but not shy, looking boldly at Ev and her father with bright black eyes. "Oh," she breathed into her father's ear, "they're so pretty. What are they?"

"Cedar waxwings," her father said. "Not rare in these parts, but not all that common either."

"Cedar waxwings. What a funny name. I don't see any wax."

"They're called that because the little red dots on the wingtips look like sealing wax. The kind they used on letters."

One flew so close, Ev heard the whir of wings beside her ear. Her father hugged her tighter. "Make a wish," he said.

That was the dream, just as vivid as if it had happened today. Ev closed her eyes to keep the feeling inside of her, the feeling of being seven and safe in her father's arms.

The bedroom door opened. "Ev, are you okay?"

"Yes, Mum, I'm okay now."

Her mother stood in the doorway looking uncertain. "John took Ian out quite a while ago. They should be back soon. I thought, when I passed you on the stairs, perhaps you'd had words with him, but he said no." Her mother looked worried. Worried and fragile. Ev thought about the happy mother in her dream. It was hard to imagine this was the same person. Ev wanted her to be the same person.

But what had happened to make things so different between her mother and Doctor Thorne?

"I...I thought you weren't going to invite him over after Saturday. Doctor Thorne, I mean." She was careful to keep her voice neutral. She didn't want to sound as if she was blaming her mother.

Nina McCallum bit her lip. "I thought so too," she said. "When you told me what people were saying, I never wanted to see John Thorne again. But, of course, that's not possible. He's one of the doctors who supervises my training. So I stayed as far away from him as I could, but Ev, he really has been a good friend. He may be the best friend I have right now, and I was miserable. I haven't felt like that since before Ian was born. Remember?"

Ev nodded. "I thought so too."

"Well, your grandfather noticed, and he spoke to me."

"Grandpa? What did he say?"

"He asked me what was wrong, and I told him. He said he didn't think Duncan would like me to be so unhappy. He said John Thorne would be a good friend for me. And then, I think he must have spoken to John as well, because, a short while after, when they let us go for the day, John came and asked if he could walk me home. And I said yes."

Ev couldn't speak. No one loved her father more than her grandfather did. His only son. If he could do that—

"Ev," her mother said gently, "I can't spend the rest of my life wishing things could be different. I don't love John Thorne. But I respect and admire him, and I've learned I can't just shut him out of my life. Do you understand?"

"I can try." Ev looked away. "It's hard, Mum," she whispered. "It's so hard."

Her mother knelt on the bed and gathered her up like a little girl. "No one expects you to be perfect. I understand." They stayed there like that for a long time. Ev felt as safe as the child in her dream.

"Mum," she said after a while, "do you remember the birds?"

"What birds, dear?"

"The cedar waxwings, that time in the dogberry tree behind the house in Belbin's Cove. Dad woke me up. Remember?"

Her mother shook her head. "Your father was always showing you things like that. I don't remember half of it."

So I'm the only one, Ev thought.

The doorbell rang. "That'll be John with Ian," her mother said.

"No, it might be Peter."

Chapter Eight

Meeting the Train

As soon as the door opened, Peter knew Ev had not had an easy time since he'd left her on the wharf. With Ev, he could always tell.

"Evening," he said, nodding to Ev's mother. "Thought I'd see if Ev'd like a walk." Until that moment, he had been planning to visit with Ev and her mother. Now, he guessed Ev would probably rather talk alone. He was right.

"That would be great," Ev said, grabbing her jacket. She practically jumped out of the house.

"But dear, you haven't eaten supper."

"I'll eat later, Mum. I'm not hungry."

Her mother yielded reluctantly and Peter allowed Ev to rush him out the door.

"Let's go over the bridge and walk along Water Street," he said.

Ev nodded. "You haven't got anything to eat, have you? I'm starved."

Peter gave her a lopsided smile. "That wasn't what I heard just now." He fished a chocolate bar out of his jacket pocket and handed it to her. Ev went at it as if she hadn't eaten for weeks.

"Want to talk about it?" Peter said.

"Well, things changed today," she started to say.

But Peter interrupted. "Better tell me later." Doctor Thorne was coming towards them with Ian on his shoulders. Ian carried the little Union Jack. When he saw Peter and Ev, he began to wave it wildly. When they met, he launched himself into Ev's arms. John Thorne smiled a little sheepishly. "Did I keep him too long?" he asked.

"No, Mum's expecting you, but she wasn't worried or anything," Ev said. "Did you have a good time, monkey?" She turned her brother in her arms to face her.

"War over now," Ian said.

Ev hugged Ian and set him on his feet by Doctor Thorne. "That's right, Ian," she said. "No more war." She looked at Doctor Thorne steadily when she spoke. It wasn't exactly a friendly look, but it wasn't hostile either. Doctor Thorne nodded as he took Ian's hand. Something certainly has changed between them, Peter thought.

"Mum's waiting," Ev said to Ian.

"We'll be back shortly," Peter said to Doctor Thorne.

As they walked away, Ev told Peter everything, beginning with last Saturday. "I thought, if I could just keep her away from Doctor Thorne, everything would be better, but it wasn't. It was worse. Talking to your grandmother helped."

Peter smiled. "Talking to Nan generally does."

"I'm tired of trying to keep things the way they were."

"Well, if you could learn to let things go once in a while, you might find it'd be easier for you."

Ev nodded. "I know. You're right. But it isn't as easy as it sounds." She sighed. "You know what bothers me now?"

"What would that be?"

"Ian will never know our father."

"Well, it was like that for me with my mother, you know," Peter said.

"That's right, it was. I'd almost forgotten," Ev said. Peter's mother had died when he was born.

"But I never felt I never knew her," he continued. "When I was little, Nan would tell me about her. What she looked like, what her favourite colour was, the songs she'd hum when she worked around the house, just little things makes you feel as if you know someone. You could do that with Ian too."

Ev smiled. "You're right, I could. Peter, what a good idea."

They stopped on the bridge and looked downstream to the harbour. Far inland, the sun dipped low towards a distant horizon. The slanting light hit the South Side Hills, throwing every small detail of crag and rock into sharp relief. Stunted black spruce caught the light as it gradually seeped out of the day, taking all colour with it. This day was almost over, and Peter was glad. There wouldn't be another day like this, a day that would remind Ev of her father as much, for a long time.

From here, Peter could see into the harbour where the *Evelyn's Pride* sat moored at the Dawe wharf. It had been harder for him to leave Ev with Stan Dawe this afternoon than he'd care to admit, even to himself. He'd seen the way Ev looked at Stan—in the way he wished she'd look at him, but never did. He framed several sentences in his mind before finding one he could ask her, one that sounded casual enough. "So Stan saw you home all right, did he?" he said finally, hoping his voice wouldn't betray him.

Ev laughed. "Oh yes. He's got a good pair of arms on him." She turned abruptly and began to walk again so Peter couldn't read her expression. He guessed that was deliberate. They walked on in silence.

Water Street was crowded with people. Some were singing "When the Lights Go On Again All Over the World" and "There'll Be Bluebirds Over the White Cliffs of Dover," songs people had sung about the end of the war for years. Now it was finally here.

"Stan told me about that trainload of soldiers coming into the station tonight," Ev said after a while. "Did you know about it?"

Peter nodded. "I didn't think you needed to know. Not today."

"Well, you were right. But Peter" — Ev's pace slowed as if she'd just hit something thicker than air— "some of those men might have known my father." She swung around to face him, walking backwards with a strange new energy in her step. "We should meet that train."

"Oh, Ev. Is that a good idea? Sounds to me as if you've been through enough today already. Besides, your mom will worry if you're out late."

Ev waved her hand, swatting Peter's objection away. "It's okay. She knows I'm with you." Her eyes were shining. She began to walk towards Peter, herding him back in the direction of the train station. "I can't believe I didn't think of this before. I was so preoccupied. Of course we have to meet that train. What time is it?"

Peter looked at his watch slowly, making a show of his reluctance. "Twenty to ten."

"Great. It's only a ten minute walk. Plenty of time."

"Great," he repeated without enthusiasm. "Plenty of time."

Ev didn't notice his tone.

Peter tried again. "Ev, remember what you just said about letting things go? Let's not chase after trouble."

"Oh, Peter, just this one last time. I'll look for someone who knew my father, and if we don't find anyone, I'll forget it, I promise."

The echo of a train whistle cut their conversation. "Listen," Ev cried. "It's coming. Oh, Peter, I have a feeling about this. Someone who knew my father is waiting for me, I know it." And she bolted off in the direction of the railway station. Peter could only follow.

But meeting the train wasn't that easy. The arrival of the soldiers gave the celebrations a focal point. The big stone railway station was easy to see in the dimming light, but hundreds of people milled around outside it. The sidewalks were blocked. The few cart horses on the road were skittish from all the excitement and needed a wide berth. Cars crawled along, not going anywhere.

"Ev, this is ridiculous," Peter said as the crowd thickened around them. "We'll never get through."

But Ev was still buoyed by the idea of finding someone who knew her father. "Oh yes we will, just watch me." She grabbed Peter's free hand. He had to steady himself with his cane as they plunged through the crowds together. After ten more minutes, they were still nowhere near the station. A brass band start to play "The Ode to Newfoundland." The train pulled into the station. "Come on!" Ev cried.

Peter couldn't catch his breath. "Ev, I can't," he gasped. "You go on without me. You'll go faster. I'll catch you when I can."

She hesitated for only a moment, then nodded. The crowd swallowed her almost immediately.

Peter looked around. People kept bumping into him as they surged forward. The fading light, the music, gave the scene a slightly unreal feeling that made him uneasy.

Then, out of the corner of his eye, he saw someone he recognized. It took a second to realize it was the soldier who'd been lurking around the Thorne house. And he was headed in the direction Ev had gone. The idea made Peter's heart pound. Wait a minute, he told himself, *everyone* is headed in that direction. Settle down. It was no use, though. Like a dog catching the scent of a dangerous foe, he began to track the young soldier through the jostling crowd. Don't be so foolish, he told himself, he's probably just meeting the train like everyone else. In any case, what harm could befall Ev here? But Peter couldn't stop himself.

The soldier was about five yards ahead. Peter kept losing sight of him in the crowd. Then, just when he was sure he'd lost track of him, the soldier's head appeared again. "Excuse me, excuse me," Peter said over and over, pushing past people as best he could, closing the gap between them inch by inch, but never enough to see what was really happening. A feeling of dread and hopelessness overcame Peter, a feeling born of a nightmare.

Then, suddenly, a gap opened in the crowd just in front of him. Peter plunged ahead, feeling like someone released from a trap. He was close enough now to see the soldier's head and shoulders, close enough to see Ev not far ahead, still making her way to the platform and the train. Close enough to be sure that this soldier was watching Ev, following her.

Just as quickly as a space had opened, the remaining

distance between Peter and the soldier filled again. Peter was only a few feet behind, but he could do nothing to narrow the gap. Don't be foolish, he told himself again. What harm could come to Ev in this crowd? But that didn't help. He just wanted to reach her, to put himself between her and whatever menace this stranger might bring. The gap between Ev and the soldier was closing, closing, until Peter saw the man put out his hand to touch her shoulder. Peter lunged past the few people that separated him from Ev. He grabbed the man by the shoulder and spun him around.

"What do you want with her?" Peter shouted. Knew he must look crazy, panting with exertion, red in the face.

Ev turned at the sound of his voice. "Peter, what's wrong?" She stood beside him. They made an island in the crowd, the three of them, people milling past on either side.

The young soldier said nothing, turning his gaze uneasily from Peter to Ev, then back again. When he spoke, it was to Ev. "Miss," he said, "I got something to tell you."

Ev's face still held the light of the hope that had carried her here. "What?" she said. "What is it?"

The soldier looked at Peter. "Is there somewhere we could talk?" he asked.

Peter nodded.

But Ev seized the soldier by his arm. "Tell me! You've got to tell me."

After, Peter realized they'd both behaved like madmen. It must have unnerved the soldier, made him speak more bluntly than he'd intended. He paused for one grim moment and then he said, "I was with your father when he died."

Chapter Nine

Joe Clouter's Story

Even in the darkness, Peter saw Ev's face turn ghostly white. He put his arm out to steady her. When she spoke, it was barely a whisper. "What did you say?"

The soldier looked at Peter in a panic.

"It's okay, Ev. Let's get you back to your mom's." Peter put his arm around her shoulder. "Follow me," he said to the soldier. But, of course, he knew where they were going.

The crowd was thinning now, and it wasn't difficult to walk against the tide of people. Ev moved like a sleepwalker, leaning heavily on Peter. The soldier walked beside them, a bit apart. Peter's main concern was to get Ev across the bridge and home as quickly as possible.

He glanced over Ev's head at this stranger. He was small and thin. Underfed, Peter thought. He barely looked old enough to have been in the war in 1942. Now Peter understood why he had been lurking around the Thorne house—he must have been trying to get his courage up for days. But how is it that he knows a story no one else has heard? I guess we'll find out soon enough, Peter thought.

As they approached the Long Bridge, Peter saw a man coming towards them. It was too dark now to make out faces, but, to his relief, he recognized the form. "Doctor Thorne," he called.

John Thorne came over quickly, his doctor's instincts altered by Ev's appearance. "What is it? Is she hurt?" he asked. He spoke to Peter, but his eyes never left Ev's face. There was nothing awkward about him now.

"This fellow" — Peter jerked his head towards the soldier— "says he knows what became of Ev's father." He didn't want to use words like dead or death again.

"Oh Lord," John Thorne said quietly.

Ev looked up when he spoke. "Come with us? Please?" There was so much pain in her voice, it hurt Peter to hear.

John Thorne touched Ev's shoulder lightly. "Of course."

The walk from the Long Bridge to the Thorne house seemed like the longest few minutes of Peter's life. At least Doctor Thorne took over. He didn't try to interfere with Ev, knowing she was better with Peter. But he spoke quietly with the young soldier, asking him about himself. Peter learned the man's name was Joe Clouter, that he'd been home from overseas for about a month. "An injury," he told Doctor Thorne. "Car accident. Spent the whole war without much more than a scratch, then some fellow knocks me over with a jeep."

Nina McCallum smiled when the door of the Thorne house opened, but her smile faded quickly in confusion. "What's happened?" she asked, her voice unnaturally quiet.

"Nina," John Thorne said, "I'd like you to call Doctor McCallum. Ask him to come over right away." Then he noticed Annie, standing in the hall. "Annie," he said, "make us a strong pot of tea."

Peter guided Ev into the front room and sat her down in the wingback chair. Doctor Thorne came over and sat on his haunches so he could see into her downcast eyes. "Evelyn," he said, "Evelyn, look at me." His voice carried a quiet weight of authority. Ev looked like someone returning from a bad dream. "Evelyn," he continued, "this young man has a story to tell. Now, your grandfather will be here in just a few minutes. I don't have my bag with me, but he will. He could give you something to make you sleepy. You could go straight to bed. You wouldn't have to listen to anything that might upset you. We could tell you later. Is that what you'd like?"

Ev shook her head. "No," she whispered, "I want to hear."

John Thorne stood and put his hand on her shoulder briefly. "That's what I thought. I just wanted you to know you didn't have to."

Joe Clouter stood awkwardly by. Doctor Thorne directed him to the chair across from Ev's, then met Ev's mother as she returned from the phone.

"Little Ian's still asleep?" he asked.

"Right where you left him, safe in bed. Duncan's father will be over as soon as he can." She looked dazed. "John," she said, "what's happened?"

"Nina, sit down."

She obeyed without another word.

"Nina," he said, "this young man, Joe Clouter, was in North Africa with Duncan."

"Oh!" was all Nina McCallum could say. Peter watched Ev's mother as her eyes travelled from the nervous-looking soldier to Evelyn. She seemed to notice her daughter for the first time. "Evelyn, dear, are you all right?"

Ev nodded. Peter sat on the arm of the wingback chair, near Ev. Ev's mother looked at Joe Clouter again.

"Do you have something to tell us?" she asked. Her voice was calm, almost matter-of-fact.

"Yes missus." The young soldier looked as if he might run from the room.

"I think we should wait for Duncan's father, don't you, John?"

"Yes, I do."

Annie came with the tea tray just as Doctor McCallum arrived at the door. John Thorne went to meet him. Peter heard the two doctors speak in low voices, then Doctor McCallum went out again. When he returned, Peter noticed, he carried his black leather doctor's bag. This he stowed discreetly just inside the front room door. Then he went to the couch and sat beside Ev's mother. He took her hand in both of his and smiled reassuringly. John Thorne stood with his back to the cold fireplace. He nodded to Joe Clouter. "I think we're ready," he said.

Joe Clouter said nothing at first, looking at each of them in turn with beseeching eyes.

"Young man," Doctor McCallum said, "I know this isn't easy. Just begin at the beginning. Tell us everything."

The soldier slumped back in his chair, staring at the floor, his hands hanging limp between his knees. Then he began. "I was only nineteen when the first Newfoundlanders landed in England. I was reared up here in St. John's. My mother died when I was eight, and after that, I never had no family, no home. Spent the Thirties on the streets, living hand to mouth. I thought the army would give me a place to belong. It wasn't like that, though. Seemed I was always in trouble. Anything went wrong, blame Joe. Like the doormat, I was. A fellow anyone could wipe his feet on. Limeys were worse than the Newfoundlanders, but no one was a friend to me.

"It was bad when we was living in the camps, but then we

were billeted in a town. Found I could get some peace and quiet in the town cathedral. Big stone building. I never knew no place to be so peaceful. So I'd go there, just to be alone. Didn't help me much with the other fellows, though, doing that. 'Holy Joe,' they called me.

"But then Lieutenant McCallum came. He wasn't like the other officers. Most of them, soon as they looked at you they put you in some kind of box. Not him, though. He had a kind word for everybody. I figured it'd be easier for me to keep clear of trouble if I stayed close to him, so I did. And things were better too, at first.

"All that summer, we'd heard rumours of a new offensive in North Africa, but we never thought too much about it. Everyone said we was headed for India. In the fall, they started putting troops together for North Africa. Torch landings is what they called them. Nobody was too surprised when we heard Lieutenant McCallum was being seconded to a British unit that was headed out. What he knew about explosives made him pretty useful. I suppose we weren't supposed to know he was going, but everyone did. I was right sorry.

"Just a few days before he was supposed to leave, I came back to my billet and found something hidden in the blankets of my bed—a silver chalice from the cathedral. They never locked nothing up in there. Some joker'd stolen it and hid it in my bed. I went to Lieutenant McCallum. I gave him the chalice and told him what happened. I swore it wasn't me did the stealing. He said, 'Leave it to me, Joe.' When he said that, I just broke down and cried.

"I guess that must've meant something to him, because

shortly after, they told me I was shipping out too. Seems he'd asked for me. Said I could be of use to him."

Joe Clouter paused for a moment and raised his eyes. "Only time in my life anyone said something like that about me, and I knew he was doing it to keep me out of harm's way. "So we set off together for North Africa. November, 1942. Tunisia. Desert, I thought it was supposed to be, but it rained and rained. Cold too. Mud—never saw so much mud in my life. Fellows used to joke that we'd landed ourselves back in World War I. But things was different for me. Everyone liked Lieutenant McCallum. Respected him. And I was with him now, so some of that rubbed off on me."

Joe paused and gave a shaky sigh. No one else said anything. It was as if his story had hypnotized them. "He tried to teach me about explosives. That was the mistake cost him his life. But it was an accident. He was the only one ever showed me any kindness at all. I sooner have cut off my own arm than harmed him." Joe Clouter's voice broke and he faltered.

"You'd better go on," Doctor McCallum said. His tone was not unkind, but stern enough to cause the young soldier to take a deep breath and continue.

"The Germans was gaining and we in retreat, pulling out of a camp. We was in a bunker and he was showing me how to wire a detonator to some dynamite. He was going to blast something. Maybe blow it up so's it would be of no use to the Germans when we left. They didn't tell us that sort of thing. There was shell fire in the distance, we hadn't slept properly in days, and I guess I was scared enough that I didn't listen too good. Because, afterward, when I thought it over, I figured he thought he was just showing me how to wire the detonator, for practice, like. But I thought I was supposed to be getting it ready to be used.

"The shells were landing closer, and I got more and more scared. He said it was after getting dangerous, they was that close, and we'd better quit. When I'd finished wiring the detonator, I handed him the dynamite. It was ready to blow, and I'll always wonder if he knew. Then he asked me to get a pair of pliers he'd left back at his tent. I'd no sooner walked out of the bunker when it blew. Knocked me flat.

"Before I could do a thing, the shells started falling right close. It was the start of a battle lasted the next two days. When it was over, we'd retreated some good distance from the camp. It was impossible to tell what had happened. They asked me if I knew where Lieutenant McCallum was." He paused.

"I said I didn't. Lied. I couldn't face the fact I might have killed him. I knew they'd think he was lost or captured in the battle. And so they did. I knew it wasn't right. But, for the first time in my life, people were treating me like I was someone worth knowing. I figured, if it seemed I'd killed a man like Lieutenant McCallum, that'd be over."

Peter looked around when the soldier finished. The silence in the room was punctuated only by Nina McCallum's sobs, and Doctor McCallum's quiet reassurances. "There, Nina, there," he said, holding her like a child. John Thorne stood by the cold fireplace watching, a useless compassion in his eyes.

Ev sat unmoving beside Peter, as if Joe Clouter's words had frozen her. When she spoke, she seemed to wrench the words from somewhere deep inside of her. "What about the body?"

"Ev!" Peter said before he could stop himself.

"It's all right, Peter," Doctor Thorne said. "It's better for her to know. That way it can't prey on her mind."

"The Germans weren't monsters, miss," Joe Clouter said. "Out there in the desert, they were just soldiers like us. They buried the dead when they found them. We used to come across the unmarked graves later on, when we reclaimed the area."

"But you knew," Ev said. "All this time. You could have written us." Her voice was filled with bitter disbelief.

There was a long pause. "Miss," Joe Clouter said finally, "I can write my name. That's about it. There was no one I could've asked to write a letter like that for me. I promised myself, for Lieutenant McCallum's sake, that I'd find his family and tell you when I got home. I been trying to get my courage up for weeks now, couldn't bring myself to knock on your door. I wasn't looking for you tonight, but when I seen you at the railway station, I knew it was time."

"You knew," Ev repeated as if she hadn't heard him. "You could have saved us so much pain." Her voice rose. "He'd still be alive if it wasn't for you." She stood while everyone watched in shocked silence. "You probably killed him. I hate you!" She bolted from the room.

Ev's mother rose to follow her, but Doctor McCallum placed his hand on her arm. "Give her a few moments alone, Nina. She needs time." He turned to Joe Clouter, who looked miserable. "Mr. Clouter, I'm sorry. My granddaughter's beside herself with grief. You blame yourself for Duncan's death. But it seems to me no one will ever know what really happened."

Peter could see the gratitude in Joe Clouter's eyes.

"Your son," Joe Clouter said, "was the best man I ever knew. I'm sorry. I hope, some day, the girl can forgive me." He stood, looking as if he was going to cry himself. "Perhaps I'll go now," he said.

John Thorne showed him to the door, then came back to the front room.

"Well," Doctor McCallum said, "now we know Duncan died as he lived, helping others, doing his job. I had accepted his death some time ago. Perhaps we can find some peace of mind in knowing." He stood. "I'll see to Evelyn if you'll let me, Nina."

Nina McCallum nodded, "Thank you, Father." She sounded grateful.

Peter realized he was about to be left alone with Ev's mother and Doctor Thorne. He glanced around the room, looking for a way out. Doctor McCallum must have noticed.

"Peter, I'll need a glass of water. Would you get one from the kitchen and bring it up to Evelyn's room?" he said, taking his doctor's bag from the floor. Peter escaped on his heels.

When he brought the water upstairs, Peter stopped in the hall. Under normal circumstances, he would never go into Ev's bedroom. He stood there for a moment, feeling foolish, until Doctor McCallum opened the door.

"I thought I heard you," he said, taking the glass from Peter's hand. Then he put his arm around Peter's shoulder. "Come along," he said in a low voice. "She needs you too."

Ev had been crying. She looked small and exhausted on her bed. Peter put the water on her bedside table and stood awkwardly by. Doctor McCallum opened his bag.

"Now, I'm going to give you something to make you

sleep, Evelyn," he said. "You'll feel a bit groggy in the morning. I think you should stay home from school."

Ev only nodded.

"This has been a terrible shock, Ev," he said. "It will take time for you to recover. Time before you can find it in your heart to forgive that young man." There was great gentleness in his voice.

Ev looked at him. Her eyes were vacant. "Forgive him?" she said. "How could I?"

"Just take this and sleep," he said, handing her the water and a pill. "We'll talk another time. Do you want me to stay until you feel sleepy?"

Ev handed back the water glass and turned her face to the wall. "No," she said. "Goodnight." The emptiness in her voice chilled Peter.

"All right, my dear," Doctor McCallum said. "I'll see you again tomorrow when I can." He kissed her forehead and turned out the light.

"Goodnight, Ev," Peter said quietly, but she said nothing. He had the eerie feeling he was leaving an empty room.

John Thorne was gone when Peter and Doctor McCallum went back downstairs. Nina McCallum sat alone on the sofa, her legs curled under her. She looked drained.

"I'd better go now," Peter said.

"You can make your own way, Peter?" Doctor McCallum asked.

"Yes, sir. I've got running lights for the boat."

"Evelyn won't be going to school tomorrow, Peter. Why don't I drive by and pick you up around eight-thirty?"

"Thank you, Doctor McCallum," Peter said as he left.

Peter passed the silent railway station across the river as

he walked to the *Evelyn's Pride*. Turning his boat homeward, he could hear people celebrating, even over the old make-and-break's racket. It was still V-E Day. A cold wind blew in through the Narrows. Where it met the air warmed by the day's sun, a huge column of fog rose over the harbour. As it swallowed Peter and his boat, he thought about Evelyn's father. A good man, just as Ev always said. Dying like that, in a flash of heat and fire, he couldn't have suffered much. The story might have brought some comfort, but not to Ev. The intensity of her reaction worried Peter. He knew Ev. A fury like that could consume her unless she found a way to let it go. And letting go was not one of Ev's talents.

Chapter Ten

The Tantrum

Ev woke late the next morning feeling groggy, with a bitter taste at the back of her throat. Everything was different. These past few weeks, hope for her father's return had gradually seeped away, leaving an empty place inside of her. Now, that place was full again. Filled with hate for the man who had caused her father's death, for the Germans and for the war itself. The dull sadness was gone and a new anger burned in her heart like the last bright spark of her father's life. I have to hold on to this as long as I can, Ev thought.

Just then, her door poked open, apparently of its own accord. Ian's blond head appeared from behind it. He grinned. "Mummy says, Ev wake up now," he announced.

"I was already awake, monkey," Ev replied. "Come here and give me a hug." He climbed up on the bed and nestled against her. Ian knew nothing about what had happened last night, of course. He was too young to understand. Lucky for him. His small, warm body eased something inside Ev, turning her anger back into pain. In spite of herself, two fat tears squeezed out. She sniffed.

Ian pulled away and looked at her, then jumped down from the bed and ran out the door without saying a word. He reappeared in a few seconds holding a clean cotton hankie, which he used to carefully wipe her tears. Then he sat facing her on the bed, studying her seriously. "Why crying, Ev?" he asked.

"Oh, Ian, I'm sad because Daddy can't be here."

Ian considered for a moment, then frowned. "Daddy's bad to make Ev cry," he said.

"Oh no, Ian!" It shocked her to hear Ian talk about their father that way. "Daddy wasn't bad. He was the best daddy in the whole world."

Ian regarded her sceptically.

"Really, Ian. He was. See? I've stopped crying." Ev stood and began to gather her clothes, smiling, although it almost hurt her face to smile.

Ian seemed satisfied.

"Where's Mummy?" Ev asked.

"In kitchen."

"Can you tell her I'll be right down?"

Ian nodded and left. Ev heard the bump, bump, bump of his bottom on the stairs. He was still too young to walk up and down alone safely, so he crawled up and bumped down.

I can't cry in front of Ian, she thought as she began to dress. Then she remembered Joe Clouter. I don't need to cry, she thought. I can be angry.

When Ev entered the kitchen, Ian was sitting in his mother's lap. "— along came a blackbird and *snapped* off her nose," her mother said, making a gentle lunge for Ian's nose.

He covered his face with both hands and wriggled so hard Ev was afraid he might fall. But her mother held him tight. "Give nose back, give nose back," Ian cried, giggling.

Ev's mother made a little "nose" with her thumb peeking between her fingers and applied it to Ian's face. "There," she said, kissing him as she put him down. "All better."

"Where's Annie?" Ev asked as she put the kettle on.

"I gave her the day off. Just the three of us."

"Oh, great."

"Ian, be a good boy and tidy those blocks for me. Yes," her mother said, turning to her, "but we do have to visit your grandmother. She'll want to hear the story from us."

"Do we have to go over it all again?"

"I think we will."

Ev groaned. "Why?"

Her mother sighed. "Maybe because it makes the story less horrible. Last night, I could hardly listen to what happened. Now, I think I can. It's necessary, I think. To make the story more bearable. To help us get on with our lives."

The only way I can stand to live with that story, Ev thought, is if it stays horrible forever.

"Will Grandmother be angry she wasn't here last night?" she asked.

"I don't think so. Your grandfather and I talked about that before he left. When I called him, I only knew it was some kind of emergency, and Doctor Thorne wanted your grandfather to be here."

Doctor Thorne again, Ev noticed, not John.

"In any case, your grandfather thought it was better for her to hear the story from him first. She isn't as strong as she used to be, you know."

Ev did know. She'd fought a lot with her grandmother, but the fights had always seemed fair somehow, because they were even, Ev's grandmother giving as good as she got. Lately, though, this was no longer true. Her grandmother was easily confused, too easily defeated in an argument. It's no fun any more, Ev thought. The idea surprised her. She'd never thought of fighting with her grandmother as fun, exactly.

"When do we go?" she asked.

"You have something to eat now. It's almost noon. Ian and I will eat too. Then I'll call your grandfather. He'll pick us up if things aren't too busy at the hospital. That way, we can be home before Ian's nap."

Ian's nap. It gets in the way sometimes, Ev thought, but it has its uses.

When her grandfather came for them, she saw how the stress of last night showed in the lines of his face. He wasn't as strong as he used to be either.

"How is Grandmother?" Ev asked when they settled in the car.

"She's upset, of course. We all are. But she's taking it well." He glanced back at Ian before he continued. Ian was looking at the boats in the harbour, not listening. "There's some relief in all of this, for me at least. Just knowing, finally, how it happened. That he didn't suffer." Ev knew he was being vague deliberately, so Ian wouldn't understand what they were talking about. That was good because her grandfather could assume she agreed with him, even though she didn't.

Ev's grandmother was waiting for them in the parlour. Ian ran to her and climbed into her lap. She stroked his head and smiled at him. Her love for him was straightforward and generous—bearing no resemblance, in Ev's mind, to any emotion she'd ever shown Ev. But that was okay. It was only natural that everyone should love Ian.

Nina McCallum went over and kissed her mother-in-law, a rare expression of affection, and Ev did the same. The news of her father's death seemed to draw them together, for now at least.

Katie, the maid, brought in tea. "Ian," Ev's grandmother said, "I think there might be some chocolate in the kitchen for you if you ask Katie nicely."

Ian jumped from his grandmother's lap and left the room with Katie.

"I hope you don't mind, Nina," Ev's grandmother said. "Chocolate at this time of day, I mean. I didn't want Ian to hear anything that might upset him. I've asked Katie to keep him busy out there for a while."

"No, Mother, that's fine."

"My goodness," Gwen McCallum continued, "imagine all that rioting in Halifax yesterday. And we had such a quiet day here. It speaks well of the people of St. John's. Even with those soldiers coming home." She sniffed and reached for her handkerchief. "Poor Duncan."

And then, as Ev had feared, they went over Joe Clouter's story again. She listened to every detail, not to make the story more bearable, as her mother hoped, but to help her remember the reason for her anger. When it was finally over, Ev's grandmother dried her eyes briskly. "We must have a memorial of some sort," she said. "But what could be fitting for Duncan's memory?"

"We'll have to think about that, Gwen," Doctor McCallum said. "But for now, there is the Duncan McCallum scholarship. And our Evelyn is a strong contender."

All three adults smiled at Ev. "I'll do my best," Ev said. She could hardly believe that she'd had doubts about being an engineer just yesterday. Now she had to, for her father.

"I'm sure you will, Evelyn," her grandmother said, beaming at her for once. "And we'll just have to think about a more visible memorial."

Ian toddled back into the parlour, holding Katie's hand. He was sponged, but still smelled of chocolate. Predictably, he yawned.

"Nap time, Ian," Ev said.

"Yes," her mother said, glancing at the mantel clock. "After nap time, actually. We'll have to get this boy home, I'm afraid."

Ev expected Ian to fall asleep in the car, but he didn't. "Too much chocolate," her mother said as he jumped up the front steps and into the house. "If he gets keyed up now, he'll miss his nap and be cranky all afternoon."

"Don't worry, Mum, I'll look after him. Ian, let's read some *Native Birds and Mammals of North America*," Ev said, picking up a volume in the front room.

Ian was spinning in the hall while he stared up at the cut glass light fixture. He stopped when Ev appeared with the book. "Okay," he said.

Their mother smiled. "Thank you, dear. I'll be in the kitchen."

With difficulty, Ev got *Native Birds and Mammals*, Ian and Melodus into Ian's bedroom. Ian threw Melodus onto the bed. "Melodus flying!" he said. Their mother was right. Ian was overtired.

"Ian," Ev said as firmly as she could, "it's nap time."

"No nap today."

"Okay, we'll just rest. You lie down on the bed and I'll read to you."

"Ian sit on bed." And he did.

Ev sighed. "Okay." As she opened the book, she remembered what Peter said yesterday. She could tell Ian about their father and the dogberry tree. "I'll read you about cedar waxwings," Ev said.

"Read snowshoe hare," Ian said.

"No, Ian," Ev insisted. "You'll like cedar waxwings." She leafed through the book trying to find the right entry, not paying attention to him.

"Ian want snowshoe hare." He stressed each syllable by pounding Melodus on the bed.

"Don't be silly," Ev said. Telling Ian about their father was more important than giving him what he wanted. He would have to just settle down and listen. She finally found the page. "Cedar waxwing, *Bombycilla cedrorum*. These lively birds are always found in flocks unless mating..."

"SNOWSHOE HARE!" Ian screamed. He was bright red. He grabbed at the book, and tore out the page.

"Ian! Stop!" Ev snatched the book away from him.

Ian burst into tears. He held the crumpled page before his crumpled face and tried to shred the paper, too clumsy in his rage to make his fingers work. When Ev tried to stop him, he hit her, hard, on the bridge of her nose. "Ian!"

"My goodness, Ev, what's happened?" Nina McCallum rushed into the room. Ev clutched her nose, tears of pain in her eyes. Ian threw himself onto the bed in a frenzy. Her mother pushed Ev gently from the room. "Better let me," she whispered.

Ev sat in the front room, listening to the sobs from Ian's bedroom, rubbing her nose. She couldn't have said which hurt more—her nose or her feelings. It was a long time before the house was quiet, and a long time after that before her mother came down.

"Are you okay, dear? Let's have a look at that nose." Her mother's touch was gentle, professional.

"What's wrong with him?" Ev asked.

"A temper tantrum. Ian's been such an easy child, I thought he'd skipped that stage."

"It was horrible."

Her mother gave her a rueful little smile. "You had them all the time."

"Really?"

She nodded. "That nose will be fine. Do you want some ice for it?"

Ev shook her head. "I can't believe he did that. With me."

Her mother sat down beside her. "It wasn't you. I should have seen it coming. The late nap time, too much chocolate and— people don't realize it, but small children pick up on the feelings around them. We think Ian is too young to know what happened, and that's true. But we're all tense and upset today, and he feels that. He can't express what he's feeling so—a temper tantrum. When he wakes up, he'll be himself again. You'll see." Her mother yawned. "He should sleep for at least an hour. I could do with a nap myself. You're all right, aren't you?"

Ev nodded. Be himself again, she thought as her mother went upstairs. Until just now, she thought she knew Ian perfectly. That tantrum wasn't anything like her brother. To tell the truth, it made her angry. How would he ever know about their father if he didn't listen? Why did he always have to have everything his way? And the book, Ev thought. It's ruined. It belongs to Doctor Thorne. He'll have to know. She guessed the set of books was valuable, but felt sure Doctor Thorne would forgive Ian just about anything.

What about Doctor Thorne? What they'd learned last night seemed to put some distance between him and her mother. Was that still what Ev wanted? She leaned back into the chair and groaned silently. Too much to think about.

A knock came to the door. Ev hurried to open it before the caller got impatient and rang the bell. Her mother needed the rest. Who could it be? she wondered. Peter? Doctor Thorne?

It was Pansy Green. She held out some books and papers. "Homework," she said, smiling. "Figured you wouldn't want to fall behind."

"Oh thanks," Ev said. "Come in. Please." As she took the books from Pansy's hands, Ev pulled her into the house. She wasn't going to let her get away. Pansy didn't seem to mind.

"Mum and my brother are resting. Let's go down to the kitchen," Ev said. "I could make toast and tea."

"That'd be fine."

When Ev realized Pansy wasn't just going to drop off the books and leave, she relaxed a little. "Great. It's this way."

Downstairs, she busied herself with the kettle and bread.

"Remember that chemistry test we did last week?" Pansy said. "They say Mr. Holloway just about exploded when he marked it. I hear more than half of us failed. We get the results tomorrow."

"I thought I'd come back to school tomorrow," Ev said. In fact, she hadn't decided until that very moment. Now, she realized, she wanted life to get back to normal.

"Well, I'm sure you got nothing to fear from chemistry," Pansy said.

A slightly awkward silence settled over the room. Finally, Pansy spoke. "Evelyn, I came to say I'm sorry."

"Thank you," Ev said as they sat at the table.

"At least, I mean to say I'm sorry you knows your father's never coming home," Pansy said. "When I knew you found out what happened to him, you know what I thought?"

Ev shook her head.

"Well, maybe this is awful, but I thought, 'I wish that had been me, finding out what happened.'" Pansy shook her head. "Maybe I got no right to go talking like this to you."

"No, it's okay," Ev said.

"Well," Pansy continued, "I allow it must be hard on you, but I knows I'd give anything to finally know what happened the day my mother died."

"Yes, but when your mother died, it was nobody's fault. I'm just so angry."

"With the Germans you mean?" Pansy asked.

"Yes. The Germans, the war." She almost told Pansy Joe Clouter's story, but couldn't face repeating it again.

"Well, that's only natural Evelyn. You'll feel better in time."

So even Pansy didn't really understand. How could she? Her mother's death was accidental. "I guess I was the only one who couldn't stop hoping he'd come home. Stunned, right?" Ev said.

Pansy shook her head. "I figure you're the least stunned girl I ever met."

A compliment. From Pansy Green. Ev smiled.

"Stan said to tell you hi," Pansy said after a moment. There was a slightly teasing tone in her voice, but it wasn't unkind.

"Stan Dawe?" Ev's mouth fell open. She couldn't help it.

Pansy laughed. "You can tuck your eyeballs back in their

sockets anytime, Evelyn. I never knew you knew him as good as that."

Ev told her about meeting Stan on the wharf. It was hard to believe that was just yesterday.

"Ev, I think he likes you," Pansy said, the same gentle teasing note in her voice.

"Oh, I don't think so," Ev said. She knew she was blushing. Pansy seemed so impressed, Ev couldn't help feeling flattered.

"Most girls'd give just about anything to go out with Stan," Pansy said.

Ev nodded. "He is awfully handsome."

Suddenly, Pansy seemed very interested in her teacup, peering down into it as if her future might be there. "So, you and Peter Tilley, you're just friends, right?"

People always asked Ev this question. She gave her usual answer. "Yes, of course."

"That's what I thought you'd say." Pansy looked up when she said this. The corners of her mouth folded into a little smile that seemed to hold a secret. What could that smile mean?

"I'll make more toast," Ev said, turning away, suddenly shy. A girl like Pansy could have any boy she wanted, even Stan. What would she want with Peter? Peter wasn't popular like Stan and Pansy. He was a brain. Like Ev. Suddenly, Ev wished she could undo this conversation and try it over again.

But it was too late.

She stole a glance at Pansy. She had an open, honest face with none of the sly lines of a liar. Ev was sure Pansy's question was not intended to trick her. But, somehow, Ev had just admitted that she liked Stan Dawe more than Peter.

Was that true?

It was becoming obvious she could no longer like them both.

Ev thought about Pansy again when Peter came the next morning. Ian clamoured to come outside with them when the doorbell rang.

"No," Ev said. She was still angry at him for that tantrum yesterday, and besides, she wanted to talk to Peter alone.

Ian burst into tears.

"Please, Mum," Ev said. "Can I leave him with you?"

Her mother only nodded. There were dark circles under her eyes. Ev ran up the kitchen stairs as fast as she could and hurried Peter outside.

"Is that Ian crying?" Peter asked as she closed the front door.

"Yes. He's just upset about something," Ev said. Peter had a soft heart. He'd probably want to bring Ian outside if he knew the truth, even if that meant they couldn't talk.

"How are you?" he asked.

"Fine. I'm fine." Ev knew she didn't sound fine. She sounded angry.

"I was worried about you," Peter said. "I know it was a shock, what you heard the other night. I know it seems reasonable to be angry at first—"

Ev cut him off. "I'm not angry *at first*, Peter. I'm angry forever. That stupid man, expecting us to forgive him when he caused my father's death!"

"Well, Ev, I was in the room after you left. I think everyone else has. After all, you can't be sure that he did cause your father's death."

So even Peter wasn't going to take her side. For a moment, Ev almost panicked, but she fought the feeling down. Her anger would sustain her. It was all she needed now. "Well, everyone else is foolish. Maybe they didn't love my father the way I do." Ev knew this wasn't true, but she couldn't stop herself.

Peter looked shocked. He tried again. "Ev, don't do this to yourself."

"You think I did this to myself? Did I start the war? Did I try to learn about explosives from my father? Did I fix things so he'd never see his son?"

"You know that's not what I mean."

"I thought at least you'd understand. You're just as stupid as the rest of them," she said. The scorn in her voice was caustic, even to her. It burned all the way down her throat to her heart.

Peter pulled back as if he'd been slapped. "If that's how you feel," he said, "there's nothing I can do." There was an edge to his voice that Ev had never heard before. She knew, for once, she'd pushed him too far. "Here's your grandfather's car," he said walking away from her.

Chapter Eleven

The Chemistry Lesson

"If I see another set of test results like this, most of you will be in here after school for extra chemistry," Mr. Holloway said, handing back the test papers. A groan went up from the class. Ev glanced at her mark. Not as good as usual, but 85 percent wasn't bad. She shoved the test into a book, out of sight, before anyone could see it.

"Now I know," Mr. Holloway continued, "that chemistry is one of the few subjects taught to boys and girls in the same class at PWC. This year, I am afraid this fact has attracted many students primarily interested in the kind of chemistry that is not in our textbooks. Clearly, something must be done."

This brought a few nervous giggles. Everyone waited to see what would happen next. Albert Holloway was Ev's favourite teacher. Son of PWC's first and brilliant science teacher, he was, as the old people said, cut from the same cloth as his father. Before the war, he had produced some of the best science students Newfoundland had ever seen, students who went on to become pharmacists, doctors, even a few research scientists. But for the past six years, his best students had gone, not to university, but to war. Ev guessed that a graduating class like this must be particularly galling to him now that the war was ending. Mr. Holloway was known to be an original thinker, and that was why everyone held their breath.

"We have a very few serious students here," he said, "and an unfortunately large number of slackers. Let's try a little experiment to see if we can fix that. Stand up, all of you."

Everyone shuffled from their seats slowly, exchanging looks that were worried, amused or annoyed, depending on their marks in chemistry. Ev stood at an awkward distance from Peter, her regular lab partner. They'd barely spoken during the drive to school and had avoided one another since.

"Good. Now I want everyone to switch lab partners. If your marks are not good, try to find the best student you can. If you have been doing well, then I suppose for modesty's sake you'll just have to stand there and let someone less fortunate claim you."

What came next happened so fast, Ev felt as if a whirlwind had spun through the classroom. Pansy Green made directly for Peter. "I'm just going to fail chemistry if you don't help me, Peter Tilley," she said with a helpless sigh. Mentally, Ev added "I do declare" to the end of the sentence. Pansy looked like Vivien Leigh playing Scarlett O'Hara in *Gone With the Wind*. She actually batted her lovely dark eyes at Peter as she spoke. It was a move only someone as self-assured as Pansy could carry off. And Peter, captivated by those eyes with a predictability Ev found unforgivable, followed Pansy without a backward glance. But Ev lost track of them then because Stan Dawe touched her arm.

"You be my partner," he said. It was not a question. "After

what you've just been through, well, no one could expect you to explain a lot today."

Ev was so surprised, she only nodded. Stan's voice was gentle, as if he understood the weight of her grief. But Mr. Holloway noticed. "Dawe," he said, "it was not my intention to have my best students clump together. There stands poor Hobbs with a woefully inadequate grasp of chemistry and no partner to cheer him on."

Tom Hobbs turned bright red at the mention of his name. Neither gifted like Peter and Ev, nor popular like Stan and Pansy, he was one of the true outcasts of the grade.

"Hobbs can come with us, sir," Stan said. "Evelyn and I will both help him." He let his voice go soft when he said Ev's name, as if making a special plea for her, a move that was calculated to play on Mr. Holloway's sympathy. It was an outrageous thing to do. And it worked.

"An answer for everything, eh Dawe?" Mr. Holloway said with a sigh. "Well, I suppose." He waved Tom Hobbs towards them and turned to the blackboard.

Everyone in the class had seen Pansy walk off with Peter. Stan had saved Ev's pride and she was grateful to him, but she sat between Stan and Tom feeling decidedly out of place. She tried not to look across at Peter and Pansy, but that wasn't always possible. Pansy sat with the textbook open to the diagram of the experiment Mr. Holloway was now explaining. She'd placed the book between herself and Peter, her head close to his. Anyone would think that chemistry was her life's passion. Brazen, Ev thought. But Pansy wasn't brazen. She'd practically asked Ev's permission. It was Peter Ev found hard to forgive. Maybe I was a little short with him this morning, she thought. Well, okay— I was cruel. But he's always taken me as I am, no matter what. How can he walk away like that now? Then Ev remembered how he'd blushed that day when he'd asked about Pansy. Maybe he secretly liked her all along.

As they began to set up the experiment, Ev found it almost impossible to concentrate. It was just as well Stan had claimed her as a partner. She was no better at chemistry than Tom Hobbs today. Stan hardly noticed though, taking over as if he were born to lead. "Run those tubes through this pan of water, Hobbs," he instructed, "and I'll explain why we'll get these results. Evelyn, can you connect the battery for me?"

Ev nodded and, turning for the battery, looked directly at Peter and Pansy again without meaning to. Pansy caught her eye, smiled and winked. There was no malice in that smile. Pansy, Ev realized, had taken her at her word when they spoke yesterday. As far as she was concerned, Peter was nobody's boyfriend. Ev smiled back, but only with her mouth. Her face felt like cardboard. Pansy didn't notice, though. She was already listening to Peter again.

"Evelyn?"

Ev turned back to Stan. She had no idea what he wanted.

"We need that battery now."

"Oh, right. Here." She was surprised to discover the battery in her hand. She gave it over.

"You can just sit and watch today if you like," Stan said. His voice was filled with sympathy.

"I'll be okay," she said.

When the experiment was ready, Ev glanced around. The class looked like a pack of badly shuffled cards. Students who normally never spoke to one another struggled to work together. Ev noticed more than one classmate watching her with Stan. Well, let them get an eyeful, she thought.

She kept her back to the rest of the class as Stan explained the experiment to Hobbs for at least the third time. But it was possible, she found, if she listened intently to the noise around her, to distinguish Pansy's voice.

"So that's how it works," she was saying to Peter. "No wonder I never got it right before."

Ev heard Peter's voice, low and patient. But he must have been facing away from her because it was impossible to hear what he said.

"You're some clever, Peter Tilley," Pansy said. That carried clear enough. The admiration in her tone made Ev cringe.

"Not participating today, Miss McCallum?" Mr. Holloway was right in front of Ev, but he wasn't making fun of her. Concern showed through his old-fashioned, wire-rimmed glasses.

Ev shook her head, not to say no, but to bring her back to herself. "I'm sorry, sir."

"She's had a terrible shock, sir." Stan insinuated himself smoothly into the conversation.

"I know that, Dawe. Get on with your work." Mr. Holloway dismissed Stan with a curtness that must have stung. Then he turned back to Ev. "If you need extra help with your work at any point, Miss McCallum, feel free to come to me. It's important," he added in a slightly lower voice, "for you to maintain your marks in light of the scholarship." In offering to help her, he revealed, as Ev had always suspected, that she was a favoured student. She nodded, almost overwhelmed by the kindness of this usually gruff teacher. He went on to examine the work of the next team.

When he came to Pansy and Peter a few minutes later, Ev couldn't help overhearing.

"What is in this tube, Miss Green?"

"Hydrogen, sir."

"And in this?"

"Oxygen."

"And why?"

Pansy hesitated. "Because, when the electrical current from the battery passed through, it broke the water down into its basic elements." She blurted this out as if afraid she might forget before she reached the end of the sentence.

"Very good, Miss Green. That's the first time I've heard any indication that you understand what we're doing in this class. Tilley, I think it would be worthwhile for you to remain with Miss Green for the next few classes."

Ev waited for Peter to protest. He didn't.

When the class was over, she almost bumped into Peter and Pansy in the hall. They made a handsome couple. Ev couldn't forgive herself for the thought.

"Oh, Evelyn," Pansy said, "Did you hear me with Holloway? He was some surprised. I actually knew what was going on. Thanks to Peter." Pansy glowed. She batted those pretty eyes at Peter again. This time, he smiled. Already used to the adoration, Ev thought.

But he avoided Ev's eyes. She recalled again how mean she'd been to him that morning. It occurred to her that Peter might be glad Pansy had given him this excuse to get away from her.

"Evelyn, there you are."

It was Stan. "Oh, hello, Stan," Ev said. His presence restored the balance. She was relieved.

"Well, we'll see you two later," Pansy said.

Peter hesitated. "I'll be walking Pansy home, Ev. Since we're going to be partners, she asked me to help her a bit more after school."

"Fine," Ev said. What else could she say? Peter seemed so eager to get away from her. Anyway, she thought, I wouldn't stop him if I could. She turned to Stan and smiled. With his sensitive, movie star eyes and wavy hair, Stan was the one most girls liked best. Who needed Peter?

"I'll walk you home from school today, if you like, Ev," he said. "There's no track practice and I promised my dad some time in the office."

Ev laughed. "I'm perfectly capable of getting around on my own, you know." Instead of laughing with her, Stan looked hurt. This was obviously not the response he expected. "I mean, sure, Stan. That would be great," Ev said quickly. "I'd better get to class."

"Oh, and Evelyn?"

Ev turned back again.

"Maybe we could study chemistry together on the weekend. Mr. Holloway's right about keeping your marks up for the scholarship."

"That would be very nice," Ev said. This time, she made sure she sounded sincere. Stan had his virtues, but a sense of humour wasn't one of them.

Chapter Twelve

Studying With Stan

"Okay, now, what's a supersaturated solution?" Stan said. It was Saturday afternoon. They were studying chemistry together at the dining room table.

"A solution that, having assimilated a maximum amount of solute, assimilates additional solute," Ev said. It was all she could do to keep from yawning.

"And how could such a solute be crystallized?"

"By the introduction of a seed crystal, causing a chain reaction."

"Correct." Stan looked pleased. His idea of studying was to memorize everything. When he first arrived, Ian approached the table with the stuffed puffin. "Puffin wants to learn," he said.

"Don't be ridiculous," Stan had replied. "Evelyn, can you do something with this kid?" So Ian was banished to the kitchen. Ev had to admit that studying with Stan was dull.

She let her head flop over onto the table. "No more," she gasped. "Not another molecule of chemistry, please." She pretended to pass out. Ev never clowned like this with Peter. It was as if she was trying to teach Stan how to play. He was completely silent. When she opened one eye and looked up at him, he had a faintly disapproving look on his face. She stood up, feeling foolish. "Come on, Stan. Fifteen minute break. Let's get some fresh air."

He left the table with reluctance.

The day was beautiful. They didn't even need their jackets. "I'll show you the garden," Ev said.

Over the past few days, Ev kept expecting everything to right itself. That didn't happen. Peter still showed up in the mornings for his ride to school, but he acted like a stranger. Somehow, it wasn't possible to reach across this new distance between them. Ev wasn't going to listen to Peter lecture her about forgiveness, and Peter, it seemed, wasn't going to forgive her for her inability to forgive. In gym class yesterday, she'd learned Peter was taking Pansy to a movie this afternoon. And he had not walked home with her once since the day things got changed around. Ev was glad she hadn't gotten into the habit of spending time with Pansy. She didn't hate Pansy— couldn't under the circumstances, but listening to her talk about Peter would be more than Ev could bear.

The garden was slowly coming into its own. Delicate green spears of daffodils and tulips studded the earth. Flowers of the *pulmonaria* peeked out, blue and pink together, against those lung-like leaves, just as John Thorne had promised they would. Summer perennials were beginning to unfurl in their outrageous first colours—red, purple and pale green shoots looking more like feathers than leaves. The garden was full of life and promise.

"My father would have loved this place," Ev said. She hadn't meant to talk about her father. It just slipped out.

"Are you okay now, with what happened to your father I mean?" Stan looked awkward. He knew the story because he'd asked her about Joe Clouter's visit when he'd walked her home.

Ev realized this was not something he would usually try to talk about. He was making an effort. The idea warmed her. "No," she said. "I will never be okay. I'm going to be angry for the rest of my life."

"Well, of course," Stan said. "Anyone would."

"You think so?"

"Yes. This guy comes to your house and tells you he's killed your father. What else are you going to do but be angry at him?"

"That's right," Ev said. "If it weren't for him, my father would still be alive. How can he live with himself? Somebody ought to throw him in jail or something. I'm glad you know how I feel. My grandfather says we should try not to be angry," Ev said. She didn't mention Peter.

"But what does he expect?"

"He thinks I should try to forgive."

"Oh, nobody does that. People talk that way, but they don't really mean it," Stan said.

"You think so?"

"Sure. I guess we're just supposed to forgive the Germans now, right? Of course not." Stan didn't have a sense of humour, but at least he understood.

"I guess you're right," Ev said. "I've just been going around in circles, thinking about it."

"Listen, Evelyn, you've had a rough week. Maybe we've done enough studying for today." Stan paused. "There's a dance next Saturday night at Bishop Feild College. A Victory formal. Would you like to go with me?"

"Oh!" Bishop Feild was the Anglican boys college. It had

a whiff of British refinement about it. The dances there were supposed to be the best, with live bands. "Yes, I'd like that."

Stan smiled. "Good. We can talk about it through the week. See you on Monday."

After he left, Ev went back to the garden. She climbed up the hillside to a bench. Stan hadn't noticed the garden at all. Ev almost wished Doctor Thorne would appear. He was the one person who appreciated this place as much as she did. The idea surprised her. Ev realized she hadn't seen Doctor Thorne since V-E Day. She didn't think her mother had either. Why hadn't he been around? Maybe he was giving her mother some time. Being tactful. Of course, he knew he'd see her at the hospital on Monday.

The afternoon sun warmed the air around her as she curled up on the bench. A dance with Stan Dawe. Ev didn't know how to dance. She'd have to learn on the dance floor. But she smiled. In the coming week, she'd be the envy of every girl at PWC— with the possible exception of Pansy Green. The idea cut right through her happy mood, ruining everything. She had lost Peter's friendship, possibly forever, and Pansy wasn't going to be her best friend now. Ev sighed. Her life felt like a sheaf of papers that someone had thrown into the wind and gathered up randomly—everything mixed around.

A noise surprised Ev. Down the hill, Doctor Thorne entered the garden. Ev shivered. It was almost as if she'd conjured him up. He carried a globe-like object that he turned in his hands. She was sure he hadn't noticed her.

"Hello, Doctor Thorne."

Although she'd spoken as gently as she could, he startled

at the sound of her voice. "Oh, Evelyn," he said, looking up at her, "I didn't see you there."

"The garden's beautiful."

He blushed pink with pleasure, looking around. "Yes, it is, isn't it? Of course, not everyone would see that yet. But you did."

He paused awkwardly, as if he had run out of things to say. Ev found she was willing to help him along a little. He had been kind the night Joe Clouter came. She rose and came down the hill.

"What's that you're holding?"

He looked at his hands as if surprised by the object they held. "This? Oh. It's a sundial. It goes on the pedestal up where you were sitting. I thought it was about time to put it out for the summer." He paused. "I hope I'm not disturbing you."

Ev laughed. "This is your garden. You didn't disturb me. I was thinking how much my father would have liked it here." She waited to see how he would react. Maybe he would want to pretend her father had never existed.

But he looked pleased. "Do you think so? I've been talking to your grandparents about a memorial for your father."

Ev nodded. "Grandmother mentioned it last week."

Doctor Thorne looked serious. "Yes. It's become something of an obsession with her. Frankly, Evelyn, your grandmother isn't as strong as she once was. As her doctor, I'm a bit worried. I'd like to do something about this as soon as I can, to ease her mind."

His concern touched her. "That's really nice of you" was all she could say.

Doctor Thorne looked down at the sundial, embarrassed. "Your grandfather has been like a father to me, Evelyn. Anything I can do to help him is hardly enough. But let me get this sundial out of the way."

He walked up the path quickly, and Ev followed. He placed the sundial on the pedestal, aligning it carefully with a notch Ev hadn't noticed.

"There," he said. "Now you can tell time all summer without a watch on sunny days." Then he continued. "Your grandfather doesn't want anything showy. We've been thinking of planting some trees. You know the memorial in front of government house, for Frederick Weston Carter?"

Ev nodded. The memorial was only a few blocks from her grandparents' house. It was for a young man who had died a long time ago, in the 1860s.

"Well, I thought it would be a good place to plant some trees. That young man, Frederick Carter, gave his life trying to save those two little girls from drowning up on Signal Hill. He didn't even know them. Everyone loved him, that's what people say. That's why they built the monument. The winds blow straight in through the Narrows there. It would be a nice gesture. Some trees to shelter the monument from the winds of the open sea. That would be all."

"That sounds lovely."

"Yes, well, we're stuck on the type of tree, I'm afraid. Your grandmother wants oaks. Now, the oak is a venerable tree, no doubt of that. In ancient Europe, oaks were thought to be the dwellings of departed spirits. Very appropriate, at the symbolic level. But the gardener in me hates the idea. Have you ever seen an oak in Newfoundland?"

Ev shook her head.

"Well, I have. They hardly look like oaks. Grow to about the height of a man. Little stunted things that never achieve their full potential. Not what I have in mind at all."

"So what are you going to do?"

Doctor Thorne sighed. "Research. I have to find a compromise your grandmother can accept. In the meantime, I can trust you not to say anything to your mother, can't I?"

Ev nodded.

"Good. I'd rather not bring her into this if there's any chance your grandmother will be upset."

Ev wanted to tell him again how kind this was, but didn't know how. They climbed back down the path to the yard.

"And how's your mother?" Doctor Thorne asked. He studied a flower bed intently as he spoke, not looking at Ev.

"She's good," Ev said. It wasn't as hard to talk to Doctor Thorne about her mother as it might have been a few minutes before. "She can't be too sad, because of Ian," she explained. "He wouldn't understand."

Doctor Thorne nodded. "He's a fine boy."

Then Ev remembered. "You may not think so when you hear this." And she told him what happened to the volume of *Native Birds and Mammals of North America*.

Doctor Thorne looked grim when she finished. "Well, I can't say I'm pleased. Those books belonged to my father."

"They must be worth a lot."

He waved that aside. "It's not a question of money. The value is sentimental. But Ian is too little to be blamed."

Ev took a deep breath. "I'm not, though. It was my fault too."

Doctor Thorne looked serious. "You're right. It was. I'll have to ask you to copy out the torn page." He sounded stern.

"Oh. Well, I could do that." It was a reasonable punishment. Ev wondered how long it would take.

"Evelyn?"

"Yes?"

"That was a joke."

"Oh!" He'd fooled her completely. He grinned. Ev began to laugh, and he did too. "You tricked me!" she said.

"Yes, I did." He looked proud of himself. "I don't imagine that's easy either."

"Would you like to come inside?" Half an hour ago, Ev could not have imagined herself asking this. Now, the question slipped out easily.

He grew serious again. "No, I didn't come here to intrude. But—" he hesitated. "It's lucky I saw you. You see, well, you know tomorrow's Mother's Day—"

"Oh no! I forgot completely."

For some reason, this made Doctor Thorne happy. "You did? Oh. Well, I have something here you might want to give your mother. Not from me, of course. From you and Ian. Just...just for Mother's Day." He fumbled with his vest pocket and produced a small velvet case. Inside, nestled in the white satin lining, was a gold pin in the shape of a slightly curved bar. At the end, a tear-shaped drop glinted purple-red in the sun. It looked a little like a falling star.

"Oh, it's lovely," Ev breathed, turning the delicate pin in her hand.

"It's a garnet," Doctor Thorne said, obviously pleased with Ev's response. "I thought she ought to have something pretty."

"But shouldn't you give it to her yourself?"

He blushed bright red. "Oh, that would be highly inappropriate, considering what your mother's just been through. No, you give it to her. And don't tell her where it came from. Please."

He looked so hopeful, Ev thought it would be cruel to say no. "Well, okay."

"Thank you." He sounded as if she were doing him a favour.

"Are you sure you won't come in, just to say hi?"

He hesitated, then shook his head. "No, I'll see your mother on Monday." And he was gone.

But he left Ev with a trace of a smile on her lips. Perhaps, she thought, liking him won't be so hard after all.

When Peter came on Monday morning, Ev's mother tactfully kept Ian in the kitchen to give them time to talk. Just what I need, Ev thought. She'd told her mother nothing about what had happened, but, of course, it was obvious that something was wrong. Stan had come to study on Saturday instead of Peter. She probably thinks we just need time to patch things up, Ev thought. Well, that isn't going to happen. Ev sat awkwardly on the front steps with Peter, wishing her grandfather would arrive early. The silence finally was more than she could bear.

"Enjoy your movie with Pansy?" she asked. There was no point in pretending she didn't know.

Peter made a wry face. "I wanted to see *Winged Victory*, but Pansy had her heart set on the Andrews sisters. Worst movie I ever saw," he said. He seemed relieved to have something to talk about.

Ev smiled. "That bad?"

Peter missed the malice in her tone. He nodded. "But Pansy's uncle turns out to be the harbour pilot. We had a real good chat at supper. Says he'll take me when he guides a vessel in one of these days."

Saturday supper! Peter was certainly getting along with Pansy.

"And how was your weekend?" Peter asked.

"Oh, terrific," Ev lied. "Stan and I studied chemistry all Saturday afternoon. It was just great."

"I'm glad to hear you're keeping up for that scholarship," Peter said. There was no jealousy in his voice. Until that instant, Ev hadn't even realized she'd hoped there might be.

"We had a nice Mother's Day too," she rushed on, changing the subject. For a moment, she considered telling Peter the story of the pin, which her mother had loved. But the new distance between them stopped her. It was the kind of secret you'd tell your best friend. The untold story left an awkward pause.

"By the way, Pansy'd like to talk to you. Got some plan up her sleeve, it seems." Peter filled in the silence.

"What kind of plan?"

He smiled his lopsided smile, the one Ev had always taken for granted. "Double date or some such thing."

I can be busy, Ev thought. Whatever Pansy wants to do, whenever she wants to do it, I can be busy.

Chapter Thirteen

The U-Boat

Prince of Wales College sometimes seemed self-contained, like a little world unto itself. But rumours had a way of seeping in from the outside. So, by noon, everyone in the school knew about the German submarine. The girls crowded around excitedly in front of Snow's to pool what they knew.

"They brought her in at dawn this morning," Violet said. "Surrounded by Canadian warships, just as the sun came up."

"Here? In the harbour?"

"Don't be so foolish. Into Bay Bulls. I'm going to ask my dad if we can drive there after supper to have a look."

"Oh my God," Doris Piercy said. "I think I'd die. How big is it?"

"Huge," Violet said. "Fifty men on board. Fifty filthy Nazis."

Ev felt sick. She remembered what Joe Clouter had said about North Africa. "The Germans weren't monsters, miss." But they were. The U-boats didn't just sink warships. There were fishing boats, even the *Caribou*, the passenger ferry between North Sydney and Port aux Basques, just a month or so before her father died. Even little children went down with the *Caribou*. She didn't want these men here now.

"What will happen to them?" she asked. Something in her

tone brought dead silence. Everyone stared at her. She didn't care. "What happens to them now?" she asked again.

"They're sending them on to Halifax," Violet said. "Maybe they're already gone." The know-it-all pride had left her voice.

So they wouldn't be coming here. She wouldn't have to see them. "I'm glad," Ev said, her voice hardly more than a whisper. She didn't wait to hear more. She walked away.

When Ev got home after school, the house smelled too good for a Monday. Her mother was at the oven, basting a ham.

"John Thorne's coming for supper tonight," she said, answering the question in Ev's look. "I thought he deserved something better than his boardinghouse fare after such an unpleasant day."

"Why? What happened?"

Her mother closed the oven door and sat at the kitchen table. "They needed a doctor to examine those German sailors. A civilian, so none of them can claim mistreatment later." Ev recognized the bitterness in her mother's voice. It was the same taste she'd carried in her own throat all afternoon.

At supper, John Thorne looked tired and a bit older than usual. Ev had promised herself she wouldn't ask about the U-boat, but near the end of the meal it became obvious that he had no intention of mentioning it. Perversely, when Ev realized this, she had to ask.

"What was it like?" she said.

He knew what she meant. He glanced at Ev's mother, who nodded, as if giving him permission to talk about it.

"It was eerie. That's the best word I can think of. I was

there to see them land. The sun came up, these fine Canadian warships sailed into Bay Bulls, and with them, this rusting hulk of a thing that looked like a prehistoric monster. It was in tow. The crew already taken off. I expected the men to be underfed, but they weren't. Who knows how, but I'm sure they ate better these past few months than people in Berlin."

Ev knew that was probably true. The stories in the papers said that people in Germany were starving. She was not sorry for them.

"They were pale, of course. Looked a lot like cavemen. Big long beards, hair halfway down their backs."

"Were there really fifty of them?" Ev asked.

Doctor Thorne nodded. "The submarine was huge. About two hundred feet long. When they came ashore, they tried to talk and joke with the Canadian sailors and the people waiting to get a look at them. But no one would. None of us could bring ourselves to say a word to them. Eerie. That's the only word I can think of to describe it. I'm sure the authorities were afraid of what might happen if they brought them into St. John's harbour."

"Sea wolves," Ev said. That's what the newspapers called them. Hunting down the innocent out there in the icy waters. Fishermen. The passengers of the *Caribou*.

Doctor Thorne nodded. "They brought the war to our doorstep. But now they're gone. I saw them leave for Halifax this afternoon."

"Well, thank heaven for that," Ev's mother said.

"Yes. We can all be glad our part of the war is over," Doctor Thorne said. Everyone ate in silence for a moment. Ev felt the same bitter taste rise in her throat, cutting through the wonderful meal her mother had made. She hated those men. She pushed her plate away, her appetite ruined.

"Nina, this ham is wonderful," Doctor Thorne said, changing the subject. He was on his third helping. The food at the boardinghouse must be as bad as her mother said.

Her mother flushed with pride. "Oh, it's nothing special. Just a tinned ham. Food is still so scarce. Maybe now the war is over, everything will be better."

"Well, there's still the war with Japan. From what I read, they may never give up." He looked grim. "So life may not get back to normal for some time. I was thinking. There's an old vegetable patch in the back, grown over all these years, but it was my garden when I was a boy. Maybe we could plant a victory garden this summer. Ian, would you like that?"

Ian was chasing a piece of ham around his plate with a fork, not listening.

"Would you like to plant a garden, Ian?" Doctor Thorne repeated. "We could grow food to eat."

"No spinach," Ian said.

Everyone laughed.

"Okay, no spinach."

Ian climbed out of his chair. He came over to Doctor Thorne. "Up," he demanded. "I want an up."

Ian never said this to anyone outside the family. Ev had always considered it part of their private code. John Thorne moved his chair away from the table, and Ian scrambled into his lap. He sat there looking perfectly content.

"Doctor Thorne isn't finished his supper yet, Ian," his mother said.

"Oh, Nina, he's not bothering me," Doctor Thorne said. He looked delighted.

Ev's mother smiled. "Well, I suppose. As long as you two don't make this a habit."

"We promise, don't we, Ian?"

Ian smiled and nodded.

Ev sat by herself at the far end of the table. Her mother, Doctor Thorne and Ian all looked perfectly happy. How could life go on like this, as if her father had never existed?

That night, before she went to bed, Ev stood by her window. It was a cold, wet night, and she hugged herself against the spring chill that seeped in through the glass. The picture of her mother, Doctor Thorne and Ian together stayed with her. She felt, again, as if she were the only one still holding her father in her heart. It made her feel heavy, weighted. Like a supersaturated solution, she thought.

As the week passed, the U-boat became old news. Now, the dance at Feild was the main topic of conversation at school. Not many girls were going, but somehow, everyone knew Stan was taking Ev. Just as she'd guessed, her social status went up several degrees, but it wasn't as much fun as she'd supposed. Girls Ev barely knew started asking her advice about dresses, shoes and lipstick. She finally lost her temper on Wednesday, when they were changing for gym.

"You really want my advice about nail polish, Violet?" Ev said.

Violet Harvey nodded, a crowd of girls hanging on Ev's words.

Ev sighed. "Okay. Here it is: don't waste your money."

There was a short, shocked silence. Then someone began to laugh. They all laughed.

"Oh, Ev," Violet said, "I dies at you."

Ev turned away and took out her gym shoes. When you're popular, she thought, it's almost impossible to do wrong. No wonder people get into the habit of being so mean.

There was no place to hide in the hall outside the gym. Pansy was beside Ev before she'd even noticed.

"Evelyn, you've been some hard to find this week," Pansy scolded with a smile. "I've been thinking about that dance at Bishop Feild on Saturday."

Ev nodded, pretending to be completely absorbed by the intricacies of her shoelaces.

"Peter and I are going too. I thought we could all go together."

"But—but Peter doesn't dance." Ev knew she'd turned bright red. She hoped Pansy wouldn't wonder why.

"Why, Evelyn, I'm surprised. You of all people!" Pansy sounded shocked. "Just because Peter can't dance, that don't mean he can't enjoy himself."

"Oh. No, that's true." This time, Ev burned with shame. Pansy was right.

Pansy smiled. "I'm sure you didn't mean it," she said. "Then it's settled? We could meet somewheres for a Coke first."

"Oh, I couldn't," Ev said, thinking fast. "Ian! I have to put my little brother to bed."

"Couldn't your mom do that?"

"Oh no, Ian always wants me. It'd break his heart. Really."

"Well, if it's that important. We'll meet you there."

Ev nodded, too miserable to speak.

That night, Ev wondered if she should break her date with Stan. Just stay home on Saturday night. But what was the point? It was only a matter of time before she had to face

Peter and Pansy somewhere. It was probably just as well to get it over with.

But the dance had lost its appeal. Under happier circumstances, she might have asked for a new dress. For this dance, she decided, her old party dress would do. Every morning she reminded herself to find it, and every night, lying in bed, she found that, somehow, she'd forgotten again. It was Saturday afternoon before she finally went to her closet. Ev couldn't recall seeing the dress since they'd moved, but it had to be in there with all her other clothes. It was not. "Oh, this is ridiculous," Ev said aloud when she'd rifled through her closet a second time. "It's got to be here somewhere." The search became more and more frantic until, finally, all the dresser drawers were open and most of her clothes lay on the floor. The dress had somehow evaporated.

It was now well after four. Ev went to the kitchen where her mother was making a cake for Sunday supper.

"Mum?"

"Yes, dear?"

"Have you seen my old party dress?"

"The blue one? Oh, Ev, I'm sure it didn't fit you anymore. You need a new one."

"But do you know where it is?"

"Somewhere where it's needed, I'm sure. When we were moving, I put it in a box for the Salvation Army with the other outgrown clothes."

"Oh no! That's terrible."

Her mother looked up from her recipe. "Ev, it isn't like you to make a fuss over clothes."

"But Stan is taking me to a formal at Bishop Feild College tonight."

"Oh, Evelyn, why didn't you tell me? I thought we'd shop when you needed a new dress for a special occasion. Once we moved in here, I was so preoccupied with getting this place under control that it slipped my mind completely." She glanced at her watch. "Four-forty! There's no point in going over the bridge. The stores will be closing by the time we get to Water Street. What about the Sunday dress your grandparents gave you for your birthday?"

"It's plaid!"

"I guess it would look pretty childish at a dance. Your grandmother thinks plaid is appropriate for any occasion." They laughed in spite of themselves.

"Well, there must be something we can do." Her mother gave her a quick, appraising look. "You know," she said, "you're almost the size I was before Ian was born."

"What!"

"Before I was pregnant, I mean," her mother said, laughing again. "I know I was huge before Ian was born. I have a dress that might fit you. Come on, let's have a look."

"Of course," she added as they climbed the stairs, "I never was as thin as you are. That bean pole build of yours comes from your father. We may have to be a bit creative."

Ev's mother's bedroom had once belonged to old Mrs. Thorne. It was a sombre room, with burgundy-coloured walls. It made Ev shudder to think the old woman had died here. But, in the short time they'd lived in the house, Nina McCallum had transformed it into a bower of femininity. The dusty velvet curtains were now in the attic, replaced by pink and white flowered chintz flanked by white lace. A cloud of lavender perfume hung over the vanity table. Ev felt she could have walked into this room and known it was her mother's, even if she'd never seen it before.

Nina McCallum went straight to the closet and dug towards the back. "This is the one I was thinking of."

The dress was flimsy satin, cotton-candy pink. It looked like something you'd eat rather than wear. Perfect for someone as feminine as Ev's mother. Not at all right for someone like Ev.

"Oh, gee, I don't know," Ev began.

"We haven't much choice now, dear. Just try it on, please?"

The skimpy dress was too short and too broad. Ev wanted to take it by the neckline and hem, and just pull until it was narrower and longer. Too bad cloth doesn't work that way, she thought. The bodice was supposed to cling to the wearer, but on Ev, it couldn't get a grip. Ev's bust was not flat, but it certainly wasn't substantial enough to support the architecture of this dress. The shoulder straps were bands of glossy pink satin. As Ev shifted to get a look at the back, one fell off her shoulder. She pushed it up. The other one fell down. She sighed.

"It's no use, Mum," she called across the hall.

"Just let me see, dear. There might be something I can do."

The disappointment on her mother's face told Ev she was not being overly critical. On her, this dress was a disaster.

"Oh dear," her mother said. Then she reached for the pin cushion on her dresser. "Let's see what some tucks will do. Lift your arms, that's a good girl."

Ev stood with her arms raised awkwardly above her head while her mother tucked at the seams of the bodice.

"Arms down now. There! That's better. Have a look."

Ev looked. The dress was still too short, but not quite as wide.

"You slip out of it and I'll baste these seams. Why don't you have a bath and wash your hair? I almost forgot about that cake."

Ev glanced at herself in the mirror again. She still looked like someone wearing a dress that didn't belong to her, exactly what she was. Well, nothing could be done about that now. She shucked off the dress and left it with her mother.

In her bedroom, after her bath, Ev took the towel from her head and began to brush her hair. It needed cutting badly. For the past few weeks, Ev had to blow her bangs out of the way whenever she needed to see properly. Now, the wet bangs were almost halfway down her nose.

Some mothers cut hair, but not Ev's. Every few months, Ev went to the Miracle Beauty Parlour on Water Street. In her case, Ev thought the name was more of a taunt than a promise. The women who worked there always remarked on the thickness of her hair and its natural curl, but she could never tell if these were compliments or excuses. Because no matter what a hairdresser envisioned, Ev's thick, curly hair had a mind of its own. Most of the time, she ended up with an odd style, and the feeling she should apologize to the disappointed hairdresser. One was almost reduced to tears. So Ev tried to stretch out the time between haircuts as long as possible. And it showed.

At least her hair was clean and shiny. She brushed it, then fluffed it a little, hoping it would look halfway respectable when it dried.

A few hours later, Ev stood in front of the mirror again,

examining her mother's handiwork. She had to resist the urge to bend her knees and puff out her chest, in an effort to become the shorter, more developed girl who might fit this dress. It had a tendency to cave in at the bodice if she moved the wrong way, giving her chest a slightly deformed look. The straps slid off her shoulders with the least provocation. Her mother shook her head.

"I know it's not perfect, but it will have to do. Look, I found this." She brought out a black velvet shawl and draped it over Ev's shoulders. It really was quite lovely. The girl in the mirror brightened visibly.

"That's better," her mother said. "Hides a multitude of sins, that old shawl does. Kept its colour too, not rusty looking the way black gets when it's old sometimes. Now your black shoes won't look too out of place. I polished them while you were having your bath. And look. A hair ribbon. Sit down and let me fix your hair."

For once, Ev's mother showed some skill with a comb. When she finished, Ev's hair was held neatly off her face with a wide black velvet ribbon, tied into a graceful bow on one side. The effect was lovely, even Ev had to admit. Pink and black was not a colour combination she would have picked for herself, but it wasn't terrible.

Her mother examined her with a critical eye, then smiled. "Not quite the latest fashion, but I think you'll do."

Chapter Fourteen

The Dance at Bishop Feild

Ev made sure she already had the shawl on when Stan came to the door. With it, she thought she looked quite presentable. But his smile quavered when he saw her. "You look—nice," he said. That fractional hesitation betrayed him. Stan was used to girls who would shop for days to find just the perfect dress to wear on a date with him. Obviously, she did not look nice enough.

Ev's chin went up. "Why, thank you," she said.

The velvet shawl really wasn't substantial enough for May. A brisk wind off the harbour made Ev shiver as they walked to the taxi stand. Stan didn't have much to say. Maybe he was sulking about her appearance.

"How's the coal business?" Ev asked, grasping for a topic.

Stan gave her a sharp look. He thinks I'm teasing, Ev thought. She met his look squarely, to show she wasn't kidding. He relaxed a little.

"Well, the shortages won't be over for a while," he said. "In fact, they're telling people to start stocking up for next winter now."

"Now? It's only May."

"Yeah. But it looks as if Japan will never surrender."

A mist-fine rain began to fall. Ev was just beginning to worry about water marks on the velvet when they reached the taxi stand. Stan, ever the gentleman, opened the taxi door for Ev. Just before they entered Bishop Feild, he gave her a funny look.

"Evelyn," he said.

"What?"

"Your ribbon is untied."

"Oh no." Ev looked sideways. The tails of the ribbon fluttered beside her eyes. She reached up and pulled it from her hair, which promptly fell forward, covering her eyes.

"Couldn't you fix it?" Stan asked. He sounded horrified.

Ev shrugged. "I forgot to bring a comb." She shoved the velvet ribbon into the pocket of her dress, where it made a noticeable lump. "I guess I should have brought one of those evening bag things."

Stan sighed. Inside the school, he nodded to a classroom that had been turned into a coat check room for the night. "Can I help you with your wrap?" he asked.

"Oh no, I'd rather leave it on," Ev said. She hugged the shawl tighter.

Stan stared at her.

"I mean, I'm a bit chilled from being outside. I'll take it off in a while."

Stan presented his tickets and steered Ev up some graceful marble steps into the auditorium. The band hadn't started to play yet, but the lights were low. Stan found a table. Ev looked around. Her mother's old dress had seemed out of place at home, but here it was positively odd-looking. The other girls' hems were closer to their ankles. Ev's hem sat just above her kneecap. I look like someone who's escaped from a ballet, she thought. She pulled her velvet shawl a little tighter and sank back into her chair.

At that moment, Pansy Green entered on Peter's arm. She was wearing what was possibly the prettiest dress Ev ever hoped to see. Green and gold brocade. Strapless. The bodice moulded to Pansy's form, the full skirt just the perfect length. Matching shoes. Evening bag. Rhinestone hair clips. Ev wished a hole would open in the floor beneath her and swallow her up.

Pansy looked around, not hurrying, knowing she was beautiful and enjoying the moment. Ev couldn't even find it in her heart to hate her. Beside Pansy, Peter looked acutely self-conscious. His suit was old, made of thick cloth, and his hair was slicked down unnaturally against his head. Even so, Ev realized with a pang how handsome he was. When Pansy saw Ev, her face lit up.

"Um, Pansy Green thought we could sit together," Ev said quickly to Stan. She hadn't thought to tell him before.

"Oh," Stan said. There wasn't time to say more, but he didn't sound pleased. Ev felt a prickle of irritation. Stan was really good at expressing displeasure tonight.

When Peter saw Ev, a flicker of a smile crossed his face. That was all, but it cut Ev to the quick, that look. He's laughing at me, she thought.

Pansy gave her a short, sharp look and said, "Evelyn, I wants to powder my nose. Come with me." It wasn't a question.

In the bathroom, Pansy wasted no time on niceties. "We got to get that hair out of your eyes," she said. She reached for the lovely rhinestone clips in her own hair.

"No!" Ev said. "Don't do that, Pansy. They're too pretty." Until that moment, Ev was prepared to resent Pansy's interference. But this generosity disarmed her completely. "Besides" — she dug into the pocket of her dress — "I've got a ribbon. It just fell out on the way over." It was damp and crumpled now.

Pansy smiled. "Oh fine." She pulled a comb out of her little evening bag and set to work on Ev's hair. "Your hair is some thick," she said, trying not to pull as she worked the comb through. "All's it needs is a decent cut. Where's that ribbon?"

When she was finished, Ev's hair looked better than it had before she left home. She smiled hopefully at the mirror. Pansy gave her a long, critical look, but her scrutiny had none of Stan's disapproval or Peter's amusement.

"Couldn't your mom afford a new dress?" she asked. There was genuine sympathy in her voice.

"Of course she could! We forgot. I mean, it was a misunderstanding." It seemed disloyal to her mother to tell the whole story.

The band was just setting up on stage when they came back into the auditorium. Even with the new hairstyle, walking into the auditorium with Pansy was a trial. Ugly duckling goes to dance with swan, Ev thought. She bolted for the chair beside Stan. Pansy followed more slowly, sweeping up in a rustle of fabric and a cloud of perfume that left both boys speechless.

Or maybe they just weren't talking. A palpable tension enveloped the table. Peter leaned over to Pansy. He jerked his head towards Stan. "Stan here thinks Newfoundland is back on the road to nationhood," he said.

Pansy's eyes widened. "Oh Stan, that's pure foolishness. Newfoundland'll never be a country again."

Stan reddened. "Why not? We were bankrupt in the

thirties, I don't deny it. But there's a surplus now. We don't need the British to run the place anymore."

Peter snorted. "Right. And how many years before people are starving again? Stan, my son, best thing Newfoundland could do is throw her lot in with Canada."

Canada! How could Peter say such a thing? "Why, that's ridiculous!" Ev said. This earned her the first approving look she'd had from Stan all evening. "Newfoundland is her own nation. The British had to take us over in the thirties, but that'll be finished now."

"And I suppose," Pansy said, "you wants to see people all over the island starving to death on the dole again, and Labrador too? Ye crew in St. John's hasn't a clue what it was like. I used to go with my mother—"

"I wasn't in St. John's until after the war started," Ev said. "And I never saw anyone starve to death in Belbin's Cove." But she remembered her mother packing extra food for her to share with some of the children at school, even though Ev always came home for lunch.

"I didn't need no outport to show me hunger," Peter said. "Nan used to give away half the pantry every week. At least Canada will give us decent dole rates so's people won't ever go hungry like that again."

"And give up being a country? Peter, I can't believe you're talking like this," Ev said.

The band began to play, finally. "Would you like to dance?" Stan asked almost immediately. Ev left the velvet shawl on her chair with reluctance. She resisted the urge to see what the bodice of her dress was up to.

"What a lot of nonsense," Stan said as they began to

dance. "Those two should watch what they say. They'll give people the wrong idea. Newfoundland join Canada!"

He was so angry, he failed to notice the amused looks coming their way. Even Ev's clumsy dancing didn't appear to matter. Stan's distraction gave Ev a chance to think. She'd never talked about politics with Peter. While the war was on, there was no point in thinking about Newfoundland's future. After the country went bankrupt in 1933, a British-appointed commission ran things. There hadn't even been elections since then. Now, she'd just assumed they'd go back to an elected government. Join Canada! Where would Peter get such wild ideas?

Stan seemed to come back to himself. He smiled at Ev. "Well, you certainly told them. I was proud of you, Evelyn." He gave her shoulder a little squeeze. Ev was glad of that. It helped keep her strap up.

Ev smiled back as best she could. Great, she thought. Me and Stan, a team against Peter and Pansy. Wonderful.

When they sat down after the dance, Ev was glad to sink back into her velvet shawl. Stan asked if she wanted to dance again, but she smiled and shook her head. Pansy was approached by one young man, then another and another. She refused, but it was clear that she loved the music. She was practically dancing in her chair.

"Go ahead," Peter said when she was asked again. "You should enjoy yourself."

"Oh, Peter, are you sure?"

"I'll be fine."

That first dance was probably a mistake, Ev noted with grim satisfaction. Once Pansy was swept onto the dance floor, an avalanche of invitations kept her there. Halfway through the set, Ev couldn't help but notice how morose Peter was getting. The idea cheered her.

"Are you sure you don't want to dance?" Stan asked again after a while.

"No, really. I'm not much of a dancer. Why don't you ask someone else, Stan? I'll be fine."

Stan looked dubious. "Are you sure?"

Ev nodded. "Really. I don't mind at all."

When he left, Ev looked over at Peter. It was hard to believe such a gulf had opened between them in so short a time. He had been staring at the table. Now, as if in answer to the pressure of her gaze, he looked at her. And there he was, the one she cared about. The one she loved. The thought was so unexpected, it left her without words. She groped for something to say. But Peter spoke first.

"You're after picking up your boyfriend's politics some fast," he said. The bitterness in his voice surprised her. What did he have to be bitter about?

"My boyfriend! People used to say that about you. Remember?"

He gave a short laugh. "Yeah, well, I never was, was I?"

There was a challenge in his voice. He's still angry with me, Ev thought. He's in love with Pansy and I've lost him forever. "You're right," Ev lied. "You never were." Well, it was the truth as far as he was concerned. And that made it the truth, didn't it?

"Excuse me," Peter said, and he left the table, pushing his chair awkwardly aside.

Pansy and Stan came back at the same time. Stan brought Ev a paper cup filled with punch.

"Where's Peter?" Pansy asked.

"I think he went to the washroom," Ev said.

"Oh, I hope he wasn't tired of sitting alone," Pansy said. "I kept trying to get off the floor. I'll stay here now."

Ev knew she couldn't face watching Peter with his girl-friend. She turned to Stan. "I think I'd like to dance now." Stan actually looked pleased.

It wasn't difficult to avoid Peter for the rest of the evening. Even when they sat at the table, the music made conversation difficult. Ev danced with Stan again, and improved beyond the point of being painfully bad. During the breaks, Stan took Ev to meet other track and field athletes and their dates. Stan introduced her as "Evelyn McCallum, the smartest girl at PWC," an endorsement that earned them both strange looks.

Ev's nationalist outburst apparently compensated for her odd pink dress, her incompetence on the dance floor, and any other social transgression she might commit. Stan's enthusiasm made it easier for Ev to like him back in spite of everything. The evening was not a total disaster.

They walked home in what was more of a fog than a light rain, Stan's arm draped around Ev's shoulder in a friendly way that seemed entirely natural.

"There's a big track meet coming up at the end of the month," Stan said. "You'll come and watch me, won't you?"

Ev had no interest in sports whatsoever, but it would be rude to say so. "Of course." Stan gave her shoulder a little squeeze again. Ev cast her mind back over everything that had happened last week, looking for something interesting to tell Stan, and dredged up the U-boat. She told Stan Doctor Thorne's story. While she spoke, that burning bitterness worked its way up her throat again.

"I read about it in *The Telegram*," Stan said when she

finished. "I would have liked to get out there myself for a look, but Dad never can spare the time or the car that long." He paused for a moment, then said, "Did it upset you, hearing about it?"

Ev nodded. "It did. I'm glad they didn't come in here — into St. John's I mean — I'd hate to have them here. I think about those Germans out there under the sea, I think about the people they killed, and I hate those men. I can't help it."

"Of course you can't. No one expects you to."

He was right, Ev knew. But she couldn't tell him the rest of it. Hating those men didn't make her feel better. In fact, it made her feel worse.

"I guess Doctor Thorne is over to your place pretty often, is he?" Stan asked.

Ev stiffened before she could stop herself. "No, not really. He only came for supper because my mom felt bad about him having to look after those German sailors."

Stan snorted. "Right."

Ev pulled away from him. "What's that supposed to mean?"

"Don't be that way," Stan said, gently pulling her back to him. "You know. Doctor Thorne is crazy about your mom. It's probably just a matter of time before they get married."

Ev stopped walking. "You take that back," she said. "We only just found out my father's dead. How can you talk like that?"

Stan held his hands up, palms facing Ev, as if he were surrendering. "Okay, I'm sorry. That's just what I hear. Look, I don't want to fight. Truce?" He was smiling. Ev didn't want to fight with him either. They were just beginning to be friends. The way things were going with Peter and Pansy, he might be her only friend.

"Okay, truce," she said. But his arm seemed heavier on her shoulder after that.

When they came to the Thorne house, Stan followed Ev up the steps to the door. Ev turned to face him and held out her hand. "Well, thank you," she said. "I had a good time."

He took her hand, then pulled her to him and kissed her. On the mouth. "Goodnight," he whispered. Then he was gone.

Ev stepped into the house and closed the door behind her. She touched her lips with her fingers. Stan had kissed her. Stan Dawe. On the mouth. Her first kiss. And she felt — nothing. She didn't know what she was supposed to feel, but there was a big blank where that feeling ought to be. She threw the damp velvet shawl on the hall bench and went upstairs.

Chapter Fifteen

The River

"Stop playing with your food, Ian."

Ian was flying a toast finger over his plate. In response to Ev, he dive-bombed it into his boiled egg. It crumpled and fell to the plate. "Egg's too hard, Ev," he said.

Ev sighed. Sneaking Ian down to the kitchen for breakfast while their mother slept in had seemed like a good idea an hour ago. Now, Ev wished Annie would get up and rescue her. But Annie would not get up on Sunday until she was called. And calling her would wake Ev's mother.

"I know you like your eggs soft-boiled, Ian, but I'm no good in the kitchen. Isn't it fun, having breakfast alone, just the two of us?" Change the subject, she thought.

"Egg's too hard," he said again. "Make oatmeal." He pushed his plate away.

Ev pushed it back. "Ian, we can't waste an egg. Anyway, my oatmeal's always full of lumps."

Ian gave her the calm, appraising look he'd just developed. Deciding whether to work himself into a tantrum or not, Ev realized. The thought chilled her. Ian was changing into someone she didn't like. She held her breath, waiting for the explosion.

"'Lassy on the toast." Ian said. A compromise.

"Okay, I'll get the molasses."

Ian finally settled down to eat the one breakfast their mother found unacceptable. Ev poured herself a cup of tepid, bitter tea and sat down at the table. She yawned. Sleep hadn't come easily last night. She'd kept replaying her conversation with Peter. What was the point of making her say they'd never been anything but friends? she wondered over and over. He was obviously crazy about Pansy. Well, why not? Pansy wasn't just pretty. She was generous and kind in a way that made Ev feel mean-spirited by comparison. I took Peter for granted all this time, she thought. Then I pushed him away. No wonder he likes her more. And then, there was that kiss. Stan Dawe would never be anything but a friend. Of course, it would never occur to Stan that any girl he chose would feel that way, Ev was certain. Where did that leave her? Not even friends with the boy she loved. Only friends with the one who seemed to want something more than friendship. What a mess.

"Ian! Stop!"

Ian had tipped the bottle of molasses over his plate. The trace of smugness in his smile told Ev this was not an accident.

"Ian, that was bad." Ev took his plate away.

His smile became a scowl. "More toast."

"You're being rude," she said.

"More toast, please." But his voice was threateningly loud. He was on the verge of a tantrum that would wake their mother. He had Ev in a corner and he knew it.

"Okay," she said. "More toast."

When he finished the toast, Ian played with the crusts, moving one silently along the table. "Here come U-boat," he said softly. Ev realized he must have understood Doctor Thorne's story.

The submarine. With a jolt, Ev remembered the dream she'd fallen into last night when her thoughts had finally exhausted her. She was out on the North Atlantic. There was a flash of light and roar of sound, and then she was falling, falling into the water. Numbing cold water closing over her head, a feeling of suffocation, then breaking the surface again. There were lifeboats. Clinging to a bit of wreckage, Ev could see Peter sitting with Pansy in the *Evelyn's Pride.* He seemed unconcerned, as if this were an ordinary boat ride. When she called to him, an oily wave caught her by the throat, pushing her under. She sank, suffocating, soundlessly using the last of her air to call Peter's name.

Clunk. Cold milk spread over the table. Ian looked away with exaggerated innocence.

"Ian! That's enough. No more breakfast." Ev swept her little brother off his chair and deposited him on the floor. She watched from the corner of her eye while she went for the dishcloth. The amount of time he spent building up would pretty much predict how fierce the tantrum would be. Ev was all the way back to the table and wiping the spill before Ian's fury broke in a wordless howl of rage. He threw himself on the floor, the sound of his scream filling the kitchen. Ev willed herself to watch without reacting. If Ian was determined to have a tantrum today, he might as well get it over with. Part of her was calm and detached, but another part hated everything about this new relationship with Ian.

Their mother hit the kitchen stairs not a minute later. As soon as she saw Ev, she stopped in mid-flight. "Oh, thank heaven. I thought he'd hurt himself." Ian slackened just long enough to realize his mother wasn't going to intervene, then continued to howl. Ev and her mother exchanged a rueful smile.

"Well," her mother said, pulling her housecoat together, "you seem to have everything under control here, Evelyn." She spoke louder and more slowly than usual, so Ian could hear her through his screaming. "I think I'll go back upstairs and get dressed."

"I'll put the kettle on, Mum."

"That would be lovely."

The tea was on the table before Ian finally pulled himself from the kitchen floor. His red face was streaked with tears. Ev continued to ignore him, giving him time to pull himself together.

"Well, Ian, good morning," Nina McCallum said when she returned, dressed, a few minutes later. "Have you eaten?"

Ian was trying so hard to look pitiful that Ev had to turn away to hide a smile. He climbed onto his mother's lap and snuggled against her.

"Ev took Ian's breakfast. Bad Ev," he said.

Ev was about to protest when her mother shook her head slightly, warning her not to argue. "Oh, Ev's a good sister, Ian. She loves you. She'd never do anything mean. You know that, don't you?"

But Ian, safe in his mother's lap, refused to agree. Ev knew it shouldn't bother her, but it did.

"Don't worry," Nina continued, "we're going to have a lovely day. Doctor Thorne's coming over to start on that victory garden. Doesn't that sound like fun?"

"Doctor T'orn?" Ian said. For the first time all morning, his smile was uncomplicated by malice.

"When did that happen?" Ev asked.

"Oh, John dropped by yesterday evening when you were at the dance."

"On Saturday evening? While you were alone?"

Her mother laughed. "Yes, dear. He expected you to be here. In any case, I don't think we need a chaperone."

Ev remembered what Stan had said. "I suppose he'll stay for supper."

"No. One of John's patients is dying. An older man. The family is driving into town today. He's going to talk to them later." Ev noticed that her mother's voice went soft with admiration when she spoke. Then she came back to the present. "How was the dance? I heard you come in, but I was just falling asleep."

"Oh, it was okay. But next time, we'll shop first. Otherwise I'll have to see if the Salvation Army can give me back my old dress."

Her mother laughed. "I'm glad you can joke about it. A lot of girls your age would have been furious. It's lucky you're not like them."

Maybe it's lucky sometimes, Ev thought. Not always.

John Thorne arrived just after lunch. Ev helped him get tools from the garage behind the house. There was even a little wooden wheelbarrow for Ian. "Mine," he said, "from when I was his age."

"He'll love it, Doctor Thorne," Ev said.

"Evelyn, Doctor Thorne sounds so formal. Do you think you could call me John?"

This request took Ev by surprise. "Oh, I couldn't," she said. "It wouldn't feel right."

"Of course," he said, "I understand."

She hadn't meant to hurt his feelings, but clearly she had. Now, she wanted to say, let me think about it, or, I just need time to get used to the idea, but it was too late. I can't do anything right today, she thought.

When Ian saw the wheelbarrow, he threw himself at Doctor Thorne's legs and hugged him. Ev felt a twinge of jealousy. She did things for Ian constantly and he never thanked her at all.

They set to work. The sun warmed Ev's back, easing the tension between her shoulder blades as she turned the earth with a spade. Fat red earthworms writhed at her feet. "This is good soil," she said.

Doctor Thorne nodded. "Built up over a long time. We'll have a fine garden when these weeds are out. Ian, I'll shake the dirt off the roots. You gather the weeds in your wheelbarrow and dump them over behind the garage. I'll show you." He knelt beside Ian, heedless of the damp earth on his knees, and explained what he wanted simply and with great patience. The child listened, rapt, and did exactly as he was told. A perfect angel, Ev thought. Too bad Doctor Thorne didn't see him this morning.

When Nina McCallum came into the garden, Doctor Thorne handed her gloves. "Here. These should fit you. They must have been Mother's, a long time ago."

"Why, thank you." She laughed. "Usually I'm the one who hands you the gloves." Ev realized she was talking about the hospital.

Her mother picked up a rake and began to level the patch they'd dug. Even in old clothes, she looked beautiful. Must be the excitement of working out of doors, Ev thought. Doctor Thorne could hardly keep his eyes off her.

Ian bumped Ev with his wheelbarrow, hard.

"Ow!"

"More weeds, please," Ian said. But he had meant to hurt her, Ev could tell.

"Ian, that hurt." Ev rubbed her leg.

"I'm sure he didn't mean to," Doctor Thorne said.

"Oh, I'm not," Ev's mother said as soon as Ian was out of earshot. "Ian's made up his mind to fight with Ev today."

Ev knew her mother was taking her side, but she flushed with shame. Maybe it was natural for Ian to fight with her, but it wasn't something she wanted anyone else to know. Doctor Thorne gave her a sympathetic smile. Ev looked away.

When the digging was almost finished, Doctor Thorne began to collect the tools. Ian helped him. "Where's the wheelbarrow, Ian?" Doctor Thorne asked. Ian pointed behind the garage.

"I'll get it," Ev said. The uprooted weeds were scattered everywhere. Ev took a few minutes to gather them into a tidy heap. Then she lifted the little wheelbarrow. As she rounded the corner, she saw Doctor Thorne and Ian approach her mother. Doctor Thorne was holding a bouquet of just-about-to-open daffodils. Ian had a single flower. Ev watched them sneak up on her mother. When Doctor Thorne tapped her on the shoulder, Ev's mother turned halfway around. They were all more or less facing Ev, but no one noticed her.

"What's this! Oh John, you shouldn't pick your pretty flowers for me," Ev's mother said. She sounded delighted.

"They'll open indoors," he explained.

"I'm sure they'll be beautiful."

"Not more than you," he said. His voice was filled with tenderness.

Her mother blushed.

"My flower too," Ian clamoured.

"Yes, my love, your flower too." She bent down, took the flower from Ian and kissed him on the cheek. As she took the flowers from Doctor Thorne, she swiftly kissed his cheek too. A look of pure astonishment crossed Doctor Thorne's face.

Ev turned quickly, disappearing behind the garage again. Before she could stop it, one hot tear spilled onto her cheek. She brushed it roughly with her sleeve. Together, her mother, Doctor Thorne and Ian looked like a family. The mother, the father and the child. All compact and fair. Not tall and dark like Ev, like her own father. She felt like someone who did not belong in the picture. She might have been a ghost.

It wasn't just Doctor Thorne and her mother, or Ian's sudden dislike of her. She'd lost Peter as well. And her father. And she had to try for that scholarship whether she wanted it or not. It was too much. She took a deep, shaky breath and willed herself to stop crying.

"Evelyn?" her mother called. Keeping her head down, Ev took the small wheelbarrow and went back towards the house. Her mother looked surprised when she saw her face but said nothing, turning to Doctor Thorne instead. "John, will you have a cup of tea?"

Doctor Thorne looked at his watch. "Good heavens, can it be that late? I'm sorry, Nina, I just have time to wash up and get back to the hospital. Another time."

She smiled at him. "Yes. Another time."

Ian threw himself at Doctor Thorne's legs. "Stay here," he said.

Doctor Thorne bent and picked him up. "Ian, my son, I have to go now."

Ian began to protest.

"No argument."

Ian stopped.

My son. Ev knew it was only a figure of speech. Even grown men call each other that in Newfoundland. But the words tore at her heart. Ian is my father's son, she thought. She took a deep breath. "Here's the wheelbarrow, Ian," she said. "Why don't you put it away?"

Ian shook his head.

"Ian, be nice to your sister, please," Doctor Thorne said.

Ian did as he was told. They waited for him outside the garage, watching to make sure he came to no harm among the tools. When Ian came out, he took Doctor Thorne's hand and they all walked to the front of the house.

"If this weather lasts, I'll be by with some seeds in a few days. We can plant peas now," Doctor Thorne said.

"That would be lovely. Now, I'd better see to supper. Come with me, Ian?"

Ian shook his head.

"Oh dear. Ev, I hate to ask, but could you look after him just while I get supper started?"

"Sure, Mum. What do you want to do, Ian?"

"Watch Doctor T'orn go," Ian said, and he sat on the step.

Doctor Thorne and her mother laughed. "Okay, Ian," Doctor Thorne said, "if that's what you want. Goodbye." He walked away. Ev's mother disappeared inside.

Ev was cold and her hands were filthy. She just wanted to wash up and be alone, to somehow find a way to feel better than she did. Ian sat on the bottom step, watching John

Thorne walk towards the bridge. There was no point in trying to get Ian to do what she wanted. He was turning into a brat.

Ev sat down on the step above him with a sigh, wondering if she'd even be able to get him into the house without another tantrum.

That was when Ian spoke, softly. At first, Ev thought he was speaking to himself, but he wasn't. He was speaking to the figure disappearing down the road. "Goodbye, Daddy," he said.

Something inside Ev snapped. She snatched her brother off the step and spun him around. "He's not your father," she said, grabbing him by the shoulders. "HE'S NOT YOUR FATHER!" This time, she screamed the words. To force them, painfully, into his head. To put them there forever. She shook him by the shoulders until his head wobbled on the thin stem of his neck.

Just as suddenly, Ev drew back. She had never laid a hand on Ian in anger. She was too shocked to even try to comfort him. Ian looked at her blankly, then turned and ran onto the road.

The car was not travelling fast, but Ian ran directly into its path. Gravel flew as the brakes connected. Ian stopped only for a second, then continued, blindly, across the road. When he hit the riverbank, he flew out of sight, disappearing so abruptly it was almost absurd.

When she thought about it after, Ev realized that Doctor Thorne must have started to run as soon as she screamed at Ian because he reached the riverbank when she did, though he'd been much farther away.

The river was not deep, but Ian had tumbled all the way down the bank. He was lying, face down, in a shallow backwater. He was not moving. The riverbank was steep and still slippery with last year's dead grass, but John Thorne flew down without seeming to touch the ground. He landed in the water and pulled Ian's body into his arms. Ev was halfway down the bank. She saw a livid gash on Ian's forehead. His face was deathly pale.

When John Thorne spoke, his voice was calm. "He's not breathing. I need your help."

Ev was beside him before she could think. Part of her mind stayed calm and detached. Feelings were for later. "What do you want me to do?"

"Take your jacket off and lay it on my knees." He eased himself down against the riverbank, making a shelf of his lap. When Ev put her jacket over his knees, he placed Ian, face down, on top of it. "Now take his head, gently, and turn his face to you."

Ian looked like a filthy doll that someone had thrown away.

"Open his mouth."

"My hands are dirty."

"That's okay, Evelyn. Open his mouth."

A small amount of water seeped out. "There was water," she said. He couldn't see Ian's face.

"Good. Anything else? Use your fingers. Check for obstructions. Dirt, bits of stone, anything that might block his windpipe. Don't be afraid."

It felt like a violation, putting her dirty fingers in her brother's mouth. "Nothing else."

"Okay. Let his head go now." He rocked Ian's body back and forth over his knees, so that the child's head fell, face down, over the side of his legs. Ev balanced on her haunches, barely noticing the cold water at her ankles. She felt more alert than she ever had in her life, ready to do whatever was needed. He slapped Ian's back firmly. Ian still wasn't breathing.

"Now," John Thorne said. He gently flipped Ian over in his arms, sliding the child's body down so that his head was tipped slightly back, face up, mouth open. "I'm going to pinch Ian's nose, and I want you to blow into his mouth. Shallow puffs. His lungs are much smaller than yours. Do his breathing for him. Let's see if we can bring him back."

Ev bent over her brother's tiny face. His eyes were closed as if he were sleeping. He was not sleeping. "Now, Ev," John Thorne gently urged.

Ev puffed. Once. Twice. Three times. It wasn't working. She began to think into the future. A future without Ian. Tears streamed down her face. "Don't think about it," John said, "and don't stop yet."

Again. Again. Again. Then, almost imperceptibly, she felt a movement. "Did you shift?" she asked between breaths.

"No. That was Ian. You can stop now."

Ev leaned back on her heels, almost losing her balance. She didn't care. Ian was breathing. He made a thin, retching noise. Doctor Thorne flipped him over. Ian vomited on Ev's jacket. The most beautiful vomit in the world.

John Thorne stood up. "You've got to help me get him up this bank," he said. "We have to get to the hospital."

Ev looked up. A man and a boy were at the top of the bank. Apparently, they'd watched the whole time. "Can you help us?" Ev asked. The man slid down the bank and held out his hand.

Just as they reached the top, Ev's mother rushed up. A

woman was with her. Ev recognized these three strangers, the man who'd just helped her, a boy of about ten and the woman with her mother. They were in the car that had nearly hit Ian. The woman must have gone for her mother. Although it seemed like hours, Ev realized Ian had disappeared over the embankment just a few minutes ago.

"Can you take us to the hospital?" Doctor Thorne asked the man.

"Yes, Doctor," the man said, opening the back door of his car for them. Ev had no idea who he was, but he obviously recognized John Thorne. They just fit into the big car, Ev, Doctor Thorne and Ev's mother in the back with Ian across his mother's lap.

"It was some lucky you were nearby, Doctor," the man said, turning back to them as they crossed the Long Bridge.

Chapter Sixteen

Between Waking and Dying

Ev and her mother waited for what seemed like hours, still in the old clothes they had worn in the garden. Ev could barely be persuaded to leave the waiting room long enough to wash her hands. Ian had almost died because of her. Might die still. It was a nightmare. Finally Ev's grandfather came. He looked grave.

"He's breathing normally now, but I'm afraid he still hasn't recovered consciousness."

"When will he?" Ev asked. When can I see him? she thought. He has to know I didn't mean to hurt him.

Doctor McCallum said nothing. Ev's mother reached over to take her hand. "Ev, they don't know if he will. And even then?" She looked at Ev's grandfather, who shook his head.

"What do you mean?" Ev asked.

Her mother's eyes filled with tears.

"Evelyn, if the brain was deprived of oxygen for any amount of time, there may be damage," her grandfather said.

"Well, how long will it take him to get over that?"

He shook his head again. "It isn't the sort of thing you get over, Ev."

"What do you mean?"

Her mother put her arm around her shoulder and spoke

very quietly. "Even if Ian wakes up, he might never be the same."

"Never?" The word was insurmountable.

"That's right," her grandfather said.

Ev had no idea how long she cried, only that, finally, she couldn't cry any more. When she looked up, her grandfather was gone. John Thorne sat beside her mother.

"I did this," Ev whispered. "I did this to him."

He leaned towards her. "Evelyn, you saved his life."

Ev's grandmother chose that moment to arrive, rushing in and grabbing Ev's mother by the arm. "Oh, Nina, I was out visiting. Katie told me something terrible happened to Ian."

Doctor Thorne explained. "We just have to wait and see what happens now, Gwen," he said when the story was told.

"But who was looking after the boy?" Ev's grandmother demanded, looking at Ev's mother, then Ev.

John Thorne placed himself between Ev and her grandmother. "Gwen, I saw the whole thing. Ian was being wilful. He ran away from Ev. There was nothing she could have done to stop him."

It was a lie, but Ev was grateful. She looked at her mother. How can I tell her I'm the one who did this? she thought. "When can I see him?" she asked. She knew only adults were allowed to visit in the hospital.

He hesitated only a moment. "Follow me."

As far as Ev knew, there were no private rooms for children in this hospital, but Ian had a private room. He barely made a bump in the hospital bed. His forehead was covered by a large bandage, but some colour was back in his cheeks. It was obvious that no one could do more for him today, but Ev pulled up a chair beside him. "I want to stay," she said.

"All right," her mother said. "In a few hours, I'll come back and take over for the night."

Ev's grandmother patted her arm. "Such a good sister," she said. "Now, I'd like to know what your grandfather can tell us."

Ev nodded, not taking her eyes off Ian as the adults left. She took her brother's hand. It was so small. She pressed it to her cheek. "Ian, Ian," she whispered. "How could I do this to you?" She thought of Ian as a baby in her arms. Of his first smile. The way he ran to Ev when something upset him. She loved him more than she loved anyone in the world, and he might never be the same.

After a while, she heard the door open. She didn't look around to see who it was.

"Evelyn." It was Doctor Thorne. Ev turned to look at him. He walked to the other side of the bed so she could see him without turning. "I wanted to talk to you alone," he said. "I think I told your grandmother all anyone needs to know for now."

Ev realized that Doctor Thorne must have heard what she'd shouted at Ian. Her cheeks burned with shame. "It's not the truth," she said. "You saw what happened."

"I saw a girl who was pushed to the breaking point. You've been through a lot lately. Too much. I know how you feel about Ian, Evelyn. I watched you struggle to save his life. Let's just leave it at that for now, okay?"

Ev nodded. She didn't have the energy to argue with him. She didn't have the courage to tell anyone else the truth.

He gave her a worried smile. "Good. We'll talk more later." He started for the door.

"Doctor Thorne, he'll be okay, won't he?" Ev knew she was pleading. She didn't care.

"Evelyn, I'd give my life to be able to say yes. But no one really knows."

Ian hung like that, between waking and dying, for two days.

Ev wanted to be with him constantly, but she wasn't the only one. When her grandmother arrived on Monday afternoon, Ev's mother said, "Ev, could you find another chair?" When Ev returned, her grandmother had taken Ev's place by Ian's side. Ev could only sit at a distance and watch. Doctor McCallum quickly assessed the situation when he came in a few minutes later.

"No more than two people in this room at once," he said. "It isn't good for Ian, and it isn't good for the family. Evelyn, you can spend the mornings here with Ian. Gwen, I'll bring you with me after lunch, and Nina, you can stay in the evenings, if that's agreeable to you," he added. Ev's mother nodded, and Ev guessed she was glad to have this settled without squabbling.

Ev was at Ian's bedside the next morning, just as soon as the nurses allowed her in. Ian lay still on the bed. Weak spring sunshine slanted into the room. It was deathly quiet. Ev stared at his face for some flicker of movement. There was none. Is he going to be like this forever? Ev wondered. How can I live with myself if he doesn't wake up? The words jogged a memory. She's asked Stan the same thing about Joe Clouter. How could he live with himself? But Joe Clouter had not meant to hurt her father. Ian was a tiny child, her brother.

She was supposed to keep him safe. What I did, she thought, this was worse. It was a horrible thought.

It was close to noon when Doctor Thorne came by. Ev was glad to see him.

"Checking up on Ian?" she said.

He nodded. "And you."

His kindness almost overwhelmed her. He'd never been anything but kind to her. The thought shamed her. "I've been pretty rotten to you, haven't I?"

He shrugged. "I understood. I had no right, intruding on your lives like that. It wasn't fair." He hesitated, then continued. "Evelyn, there's something I want you to know. I always intended to go back to Labrador after my mother died. I'd even written to the Grenfell Mission. When I met your mother, I got distracted. But I realize now how selfish I've been. If what happened to Ian is anyone's fault, it's mine. I'm wanted at the hospital in Battle Harbour. I'll go back to Labrador in the fall."

A few weeks ago, Ev would have welcomed this news. Now, she chose her words very carefully. "What you heard me say to Ian on Sunday was wrong."

"Evelyn, this isn't about right and wrong."

"Please listen. What Ian said, when he called you Daddy, it was...it was like a seed crystal. You know? Like when you drop a seed crystal into a supersaturated solution and it starts a chain reaction. Everything came together and I just couldn't stand it anymore. Do you understand?"

He nodded.

Ev took a deep breath. The wrong words could ruin everything now. "Doctor Thorne, please don't go back to Labrador. You'll break my mother's heart."

"You really think so?" The idea of breaking her mother's heart made him ridiculously happy. Ev had to smile.

"Yes. I really do."

"But how do you feel?"

"I think she deserves to be happy." Ev sighed. "So much has gone wrong for me lately. It doesn't have that much to do with you. I've been angry, ever since that man Joe Clouter came. I thought what he did made him a terrible person. And now, I've done something worse. I've been sitting here thinking about that."

"Evelyn, you're not a terrible person. Everyone does things they regret."

"This is worse." Ev said. "This is unforgivable."

Doctor Thorne walked over and put his hand on her shoulder. "Try not to be too hard on yourself."

"Why shouldn't I be? I've been hard on everyone else."

"Right and wrong aren't always easy to tell apart. That's hard to accept when you're young. You wanted Joe Clouter to be a bad person, because that helped make some sense of your father's death. But he isn't a bad person, and neither are you. I watched you struggle with your anger, wishing I could do something to help, but I knew I was just part of the problem as far as you were concerned."

"I don't think that now," Ev protested.

He smiled. "No, I know. I'm glad."

"Does Grandpa know what really happened to Ian?"

"No. I haven't said anything to anyone. You're the only one who can decide what to do about that, Ev."

"Oh, I don't know." Ev's voice dropped to a whisper. "It would be like Joe Clouter coming to us. That must have been hard for him, and look what I did. Now, I'll probably never have a chance to tell him I understand."

John blushed. "I might be able to find him if it came to that." His voice sounded funny.

Ev gave him a hard look. "You know where he is, don't you?"

"He's working in the hospital boiler room."

"How did that happen?"

"It isn't hard to convince people to employ returning soldiers."

"And you did the convincing?"

He blushed again. "I pulled a few strings. Your grandfather and I thought Joe deserved a break."

Ev considered. "I guess he does. Maybe one day you'll show me how to find him."

John Thorne smiled. "Give yourself some time, Evelyn. He'll be there."

When her grandmother came soon after, Ev went home, supposedly to rest. But without Ian, the Thorne house was too big, the quiet too loud. Ev did not rest. Instead, she wandered from room to room, wondering if Ian would ever play here again. She thought about Peter, and how she'd pushed him away. She wished she could talk to him now. Maybe he'd come after school. But he didn't. Ev couldn't stand the thought of sitting around, waiting for Peter. At four-thirty she walked back to the hospital.

Her mother was alone at Ian's bedside. She smiled when Ev came in. "He talked a little in his sleep while you were gone," she said.

"What did he say?"

"He called for John. He called for you. He's been moving

his hands too. Pull up a chair." The strain of staying with Ian showed in her mother's face.

"Mum, you look so tired. Why don't you get a cup of tea?"

Her mother smiled. "Maybe I will."

Ev took her mother's place by Ian's bedside. His breathing was calm, his face peaceful. Ev was tired too. She'd hardly slept since Sunday. She would just put her head down on the mattress beside Ian for a minute and...

She must have dozed because she thought she heard Ian's voice. "What doing, Ev?" She raised her head. He was looking at her, curious, alert.

"Ian!" She tried not to shout. "Oh, Ian, you're awake. How do you feel?"

"Head hurts," Ian said. He tried to raise his head off the pillow, but couldn't. He moaned.

"Shhh. It's okay. Everything's going to be okay. Oh, Ian, I love you so much." Tears spilled down Ev's cheeks. She couldn't stop them. "Can you lie still while I get Mum? She wants to see you too."

"Yes."

In the hall, Ev almost ran into John Thorne. He looked startled when he saw her face. "What is it?"

"He's awake."

"I'll find your mother. You go back to Ian." He was halfway down the hall before the words were out.

When they arrived, Ian was already drifting off to sleep. "Ian," John said, "don't go to sleep yet. Let's play some games with this flashlight. See?" He shone the light in Ian's eyes. Ian whimpered, but John smiled. "His pupils are dilating normally. That's a good sign. He should recover quickly now."

When Ev's grandfather arrived, he insisted she go back to

school the next day. "I'll hire Mrs. Bursey to stay with Ian. That way, he'll always have someone he knows with him." Ev began to protest, but her grandfather cut her off. "You can come as soon as school is over. The hospital's close. Your mother won't complete her upgrading this year if she takes much more time off, and you have that scholarship exam," he said.

Ev realized there was no point in arguing. She would have to face school again at some point.

St. John's was a small city. Everyone at school would know why Ev had been away for two days. She wondered how much they would know about what really happened.

"I'm some sorry to hear about your little brother, Ev," Doris said outside of Snow's the next day. "How did it happen?"

Ev searched Doris's face. There was no hidden malice in the question. But suddenly she saw Ian, limp as a rag doll, lying face down in dirty water.

"I don't want to talk about it," she said, and she turned and fled. No one else asked after that.

At chemistry, Ev hesitated outside the door. I could skip off, she thought, just show up at the hospital. No one would blame me. But she steadied herself and plunged ahead. She took her place, being careful not to glance at Peter and Pansy. Stan and Tom were already seated. "I'm sorry about your brother, Evelyn," Stan said. Ev was grateful for the sincerity in his voice.

"I'm going to the hospital after class to see him. Come with me?" Ev asked.

Stan shook his head. "Hospitals make me queasy. Anyway, that big track meet's coming up this weekend."

"Maybe tomorrow?"

"This is a really big event, Ev. I'll be at it every day. I'm counting on you to be there too. You understand, don't you?"

"Sure I do." So much for sincerity. How could Ian mean less than a track meet? Maybe that was unfair. Stan barely knew Ian.

The class she had been dreading flew by. For the first time since the accident, Ev took real pleasure in something outside Ian's hospital room. She was so absorbed in her work, she even forgot that Peter and Pansy were in the room. Stan bolted out the door when class was over, his mind already on the coming track meet. Ev found Peter with Pansy in the hall. Not the ideal situation, but she wasn't likely to find him alone any more. And she just had to talk to him.

"You haven't asked me about Ian, Peter," she said. Her tone was not accusatory. She just wanted to know why.

Peter looked embarrassed. "Nan tells me," he said.

"Oh, right." Of course. Mrs. Bursey would. Suddenly, Ev couldn't think of anything else to say.

"I got to get some homework from Vi," Pansy said suddenly. She seemed to be giving them a chance to talk alone. But neither could think of anything to say. Peter studied his boots and shifted his books. Say something, Ev commanded herself.

"Peter—"

"I—" They both spoke at once, then stopped.

"It's okay," Ev said. "You first."

"I found a place to tie up the boat on the north side, not too far from the dry dock. The streetcar runs nearby. I figure, with Ian in hospital and all, your grandfather's got enough to worry about. I won't be needing a ride to school."

Ev almost panicked. "But it isn't trouble. Really, Peter, you don't have to do this."

"I already spoke to your grandfather." His tone was final. Ev knew if she said anything else, it would sound like begging, so she fell silent. But she couldn't bring herself to say goodbye. Surely Peter had something more to say to her. The pause stretched into a long, embarrassing silence. Finally, Peter spoke. "I may not have to worry about the boat much longer in any case. I think I found a buyer for her."

Ev was stricken. "Oh, Peter! You love that boat. You shouldn't have to give her up."

For some reason, this made Peter angry. "What odds? She was never intended for me. Now I got to be going. Goodbye."

Ev swung around before Peter could see her face, and left blindly, in the wrong direction. He isn't even my friend now, she thought.

A warm breeze brushed Ev's cheek as she walked towards the hospital. The buds on the trees were opening now. She didn't see them. All that time when Ian was unconscious, Ev had waited for Peter to come to her. Over and over she'd imagined Peter putting his hand on her shoulder, comforting her, telling her everything would be okay. That never happened. It wasn't like Peter to stay angry. I've been so stupid and unkind, Ev thought. Maybe I deserve this.

Chapter Seventeen

Ev's Decision

When Ev arrived at the hospital, her grandfather met her in the hall. As soon as she saw him, she knew something was wrong.

"What is it?" she asked.

"Don't be alarmed, Evelyn," he said, then he glanced around. This was not the place for a private conversation. "Come to my office so we can talk."

Doctor McCallum's office was perfectly neat and tidy. They both sat down. Her grandfather ran his hand through his silver hair. "Ian's developed a slight fever. He probably picked up a mild infection from the river. The Waterford's none too clean. Nothing to worry about, but we'll keep him here until it's gone."

"Will he be okay?"

"Yes, I'm almost certain."

Ev let out a breath she hadn't even known she was holding. "Oh good. I don't know what I'd do if anything else happened to Ian."

Her grandfather searched her face. "This has been hard on you, Evelyn. Are you okay?"

Ev nodded. "As long as Ian is."

"And how's school? Getting ready for that scholarship exam?"

"Oh, Grandpa," she said, "I'm not sure I want to take that exam."

Her grandfather was so surprised, he didn't speak, so she hurried on. "I'm not sure I want to be an engineer. I know I was supposed to, for my father. Do you think he'd be disappointed?"

Her grandfather stayed silent for a moment, but a strange smile came over his face. "Evelyn," he said at last, "I'm going to do something I never thought I'd do. I'm going to break a promise I made to your father when he was about your age."

"Should you do that?"

"Yes, I think I should. Your father didn't always want to be an engineer. Did you know that?"

"No. He never told me."

"I don't think he told anyone, unless he told your mother. When he was your age, he wanted to be a doctor, like me."

"Really? Then why didn't he?"

"Well, I started taking him out on calls, to give him some idea of medicine. Then I was called out on an emergency. A man had taken some fingers off with a hatchet. I brought Duncan along, but ended up looking after him as well."

"Why? What happened?"

"He fainted. He didn't have the stomach for it, Ev. Some don't. He asked me never to tell anyone, and I haven't until today. But he always wished he could have been a doctor."

"And I never knew," Ev said. Just for a moment, her father seemed so near. She thought if she turned, she'd find him standing in the doorway behind her. Like a flame, the feeling flickered, then went out. So many things she would never know about him. "What about Grandmother?" Ev asked. "Will she be disappointed?"

170

"If you decide that's what you want, you can leave her to me."

Ev found Ian fretful, restless in his bed. "How is he?" Ev asked, but she avoided Mrs. Bursey's eyes. Peter's grandmother would be too quick to read feelings Ev couldn't hide yet.

"Just a touch feverish," she said. "Nothing to worry about if he's no worse than this."

"Bring Melodus," Ian whimpered.

Ev kissed his forehead. It felt hot. "I promise," she said.

When Ev arrived at the hospital the next day, she dug into her book bag and removed a package, carefully wrapped in scarves. She sat Melodus on the bedside table.

"Well now, look at that," Mrs. Bursey said. "Your sister's brought your friend to visit." She smiled at Ev. "His fever's down today. Almost gone." She stood up. "You don't mind if I slips down to Maternity for a minute, do you, child? There's a new baby there today, daughter of a young woman I borned myself. I've been wanting all day to visit with them."

"Of course not. Ian and I will be fine, won't we, monkey?" As Mrs. Bursey left, Ev kissed his forehead. It felt cool.

"Give Melodus to me," Ian said. He sounded very grown up.

"Okay, Ian, but no rough stuff." Ev handed the bird over. The bed covers were rumpled. As Ev tidied them, a small object fell out of the blanket. She picked it up. It was a bubble wand, carved from a single piece of solid wood. Only one person she knew could carve like that. Ev clutched the wood, her heart pounding. "Ian," she said, "where did this come from?"

Ian smiled. "Peter maked it," he said.

"Did Mrs. Bursey give it to you?"

Ian shook his head. "Peter bringed it."

"When?" she asked, "How many times?" She stopped. It was useless. Ian couldn't count. So Peter didn't desert Ian, she thought. Only me.

On Saturday morning, Ev convinced her mother to sleep in. When she arrived at the hospital, she found her grandmother with Ian, sitting at his bedside with a glass of apple juice. The older woman looked up sharply when the door opened.

"Yes," she said, "what do you want?"

Ev was confused. "I came to see Ian," she said.

Her grandmother gave her a cold look. "If you mean Doctor McCallum, young lady, you'll find him in his office." She turned back to the apple juice. "Come along, Duncan," she said, "just one more sip for Mother."

The room seemed to shift. Ev put her hand on the door frame to steady herself. "Grandmother," she said, "it's me, Evelyn."

Her grandmother looked at her again. Her eyes seemed to come into focus. "Oh, Evelyn. Look, Ian, here's your sister." She didn't seem to realize what she'd just said. It frightened Ev too much to mention. Grandmother made some kind of mistake, that was all. She was relieved when her grandfather entered the room a few minutes later.

"Oh, Evelyn, I'm glad you're here. Suppose I just drive your grandmother home and come right back. John and I have decided this boy's too well to be in hospital. I'll drive you both home, surprise your mother before she has a chance to get here today."

"Oh, that would be great. Isn't that great, Ian? You're coming home today."

When her grandparents left, Ev knew she should feel nothing but happiness. But as she gathered Ian's few belongings, she found the bubble wand again. Rubbing her fingers over the smooth carved wood, she allowed herself a little disappointment too. Since she'd found the toy, she'd hoped to catch Peter at the hospital. Just to talk to him alone again. Now, even that hope was gone.

A few hours later, Ian was installed on the couch in the front room of the Thorne house with Melodus in his lap. But for the scar on his forehead, Ev could almost believe nothing had happened. The battered volumes of *Native Birds and Mammals of North America* sat on the end table.

"Read book, Ev?" Ian asked. It wasn't a demand.

"Sure, Ian. What would you like?"

"You pick," he said.

Ev couldn't remember the last time he'd let her choose. She opened volume one, angling it so that Ian wouldn't see the torn page, took a deep breath and began to read. "Cedar waxwing, *Bombycilla cedrorum*." After, she found pictures of cedar waxwings on a colour plate of birds. "Now," she said, "I'm going to tell you a story about Daddy and me and the cedar waxwings."

When she finished, Ian said, "Tell story again."

Ev laughed and hugged him.

Chapter Eighteen

Swedish Mountain Ash

On Monday morning, Ev made a quick trip to the principal's office before classes to tell Mr. Warren she would not be writing the exam.

"Why, Evelyn, this is sudden. Are you sure? I know the committee saw you as a strong contender."

"I'm positive, Mr. Warren. I don't want to be an engineer. I've talked it over with my grandfather and he agrees."

"As long as you're certain."

"I am." Ev began to leave, but turned back. "Mr. Warren, there's just one more thing. I wonder, would it be necessary to make this public? My withdrawal from the exam, I mean."

"No, I don't see why we need to. Of course, when the winner is announced, people may think you lost the scholarship."

"Oh, I don't care about that. It's just that so much has happened in the last few weeks, I don't want to answer a lot of questions." Especially, Ev thought as she left, from Peter Tilley and Stan Dawe.

Coming out of the principal's office, Ev was confronted by the display case in the main hall. She'd been too distracted to notice it on her way in. It was decked with red, white and blue bunting and filled with trophies and ribbons. The track meet!

It happened on the weekend. She hadn't given it a thought. But Ian came home. Stan would have to understand.

Stan did not. He was waiting outside Ev's classroom at noon. They stood together uncomfortably, saying nothing until the hall emptied out and they could talk.

"How was the track meet, Stan?" Ev asked. Might as well get it over with.

"I broke the city record for the one hundred yard dash," Stan said. He sounded angry about it.

"Oh great."

"Evelyn, you were supposed to be there, remember?"

"Look, Stan, Ian came home from the hospital. I forgot, okay?"

"That was more important to you than my track meet?" Stan asked.

Of course it was! Ev thought. She was going to say it, but Stan looked genuinely hurt. There was no point in being mean. "Stan," she said, "I don't think we have that much in common. Lots of girls are dying to go out with you."

Stan looked as if he couldn't believe what she'd said. Then his face hardened and the hurt look disappeared. "If that's really what you want," he said. He turned to go. "I thought a girl like you would be glad to go out with me." There was bitterness in this parting shot.

Ev had been walking away, but this stopped her cold. "What do you mean, a girl like me?"

He came back. "You know. A brain who wears funny dresses to dances. Who's going to go out with someone like you?" His voice was mean now.

"Well, if you felt that way, why did you ask me out to begin with?" Ev couldn't stop herself from asking.

"I figure university will be blocked with girls like you. Thought maybe I could get used to it. So long, Evelyn."

Ev felt as though she'd been hit just under her rib cage. She hugged herself to ease the pain. *At least I know I was right to stop seeing him,* she thought. *In a few days, I'll probably be glad he did that. In a few days.* Now, *Stan will probably think I withdrew from the exam just to avoid him.* The idea galled her so much that she almost reconsidered. But that would be silly. She didn't want the scholarship.

Ev wasn't surprised to see Doctor Thorne's car in front of the house when she came home that afternoon, but she didn't expect to find him in his gardening clothes. He smiled and waved her towards the back garden. "Come see what I've got," he said.

Leaning against the garage were six spindly trees about the same height as Ev, their roots wrapped in burlap. Ev looked at the leaves. "Oaks," she said. *So Grandmother had won. Ev wasn't surprised. Grandmother generally did.*

John Thorne laughed. "No, they're not."

"What do you mean?" Ev asked.

"Well, it took some research. Most reference books don't even include them. Even after I knew what I wanted, they weren't easy to find. I had to drive all the way to a farm in Topsail. I'm glad they fooled you."

"But what are they?"

"*Sorbus intermedia brouwers.* Swedish mountain ash. They're a kind of dogberry. I found a picture of one fully grown. They only reach about twenty feet, but they're lovely, Ev. Pale green leaves, white flowers. Perfect for this climate. They'll be strong and healthy. But the leaves look like oak."

"So, do we tell Grandmother?"

He looked sheepish. "That's what I wanted to ask you."

Ev studied the little trees. "She isn't exactly herself any more, is she?" The secret she couldn't bring herself to tell anyone else slipped out so easily.

He looked serious. "You've noticed."

Ev told him what happened in the hospital on Saturday morning.

He sighed when she finished. "I don't think your grandfather realizes how serious her problem is yet. I have to talk to him soon."

When he said this, Ev felt something so unlike anything she had ever felt for her grandmother, she could not name it at first. Then she realized. It was pity. "As far as she knows," Ev said, "these trees are just what she wanted. Why don't we leave it that way?"

"That's what I thought, too."

Ev smiled. Sometimes, the truth was not the most important thing. But only sometimes.

"My mother should know what happened to Ian," she said. "Why it happened. It doesn't feel right to keep it from her. When it's time to tell her, will you help me?"

"I would be happy to."

"Thank you. And remember you said you'd take me to Joe Clouter?" Ev asked. "I think I'll be ready soon."

He gave her such a look of pure admiration that she had to pretend to study the small trees to hide her embarrassment.

"They're writing the exam for the scholarship right now," Ev said. "The winner will be announced at an assembly tomorrow. Grandpa and Grandmother are presenting the award." She wondered what Peter and Stan had thought when she hadn't shown up to take the exam. John Thorne noticed her frown.

"Are you sorry you withdrew?" he asked.

Ev shook her head. "No. I've been thinking. When I helped you with Ian, when he was in the river, it was really scary, but there was something about it that made me feel, I don't know how to say it...more like myself than I've ever felt before."

"You handled it wonderfully. I've been meaning to tell you that. I've seen medical students fall apart under less pressure."

"Really? Do you think I could be a doctor?"

John Thorne gave the question serious thought. "Yes, I do."

Ev smiled. "All this time, I thought I had to be an engineer because of my father, but now, I think that's what I'd like to do."

"Well, I think that's a fine decision."

Ev sighed. "Yes. There's only one thing I feel bad about. Montreal. It sounded so exotic."

"Your grandfather did his medical training at McGill, Evelyn. So did I. There's no reason why you shouldn't go to Montreal."

Ev studied her shoes. "Without the scholarship, I'm not sure we can afford it. Mum doesn't like to ask my grandparents for money."

"Evelyn, an old bachelor like me doesn't need much money. If it comes to that, I'd be happy to help."

"Really?"

"Yes."

Ev wasn't sure what her mother would say, but she was touched. "Thank you, John."

It was the first time she'd called him by his name. He looked pleased. He said nothing, but a comfortable silence settled between them. Ev looked around the garden. She'd scarcely glanced at it since Ian's accident. Now, it was transformed. Daffodils and tulips blazed in the sun. A sudden movement in the trees near the sundial caught her eye.

"Look!" she said.

John followed her gaze. "A cedar waxwing. Just one? That's odd. They almost always flock."

The bird flew to a branch at the edge of the trees and looked directly at Ev with saucy black eyes. When Ev edged nearer, it turned and flew away. But it left her with the feeling her father was near. Make a wish, she thought. But what would she wish for? With a shock, she realized she couldn't wish her father back. In the time since his death, life had grown over his absence, in the way that healthy flesh grows over a wound. He lived now only in the memories of those who'd loved him. Ev spoke very softly, so John Thorne wouldn't hear her. "Goodbye, Daddy," she said.

She turned and looked at John, bent over his little trees. He was a shy, awkward man, possessed of an unlimited store of useless information; a kind, caring person who would try to make them happy. He wasn't her father. He never would be. That was okay.

Ev looked at the trees again. "When do we plant them?"

"Sun up, Sunday morning. No one will be around. It should be very private. We'll have to keep them watered this summer while they make roots. I spoke to the sexton at St.

Thomas's about using their tap. Lots of water to haul if it's dry. Will you help me?"

"Yes, I will."

"Good. It's a fitting place for these trees, considering the kind of man your father was."

Ev looked at him with curiosity. "Did you know my father?"

"Well, of course. Our fathers were good friends. Duncan was five years younger, so we didn't know each other well. And you know how it is. I was a plodder. I spent most of my time alone with my books. Duncan was the golden boy. Everyone wanted to be his friend. He was the one who could do anything."

But that wasn't true. Ev thought about telling John her grandfather's story. She decided it could wait. They would have time to talk about her father. Lots of time.

The next morning, Ev seriously considered staying home. But then, everyone would think she'd lost the scholarship for sure. In assembly, as she took her place in the audience with her class, the whispers started. Everyone seemed to be staring at her.

Her mother and grandparents were on the stage. Mr. Warren brought Peter and Stan out. The two boys sat down. When Stan found her in the audience, he looked smug. But Peter looked furious.

The speeches started. Mr. Warren said nice things about her father. Then her grandfather rose. Standing there, before such a large crowd, Ev suddenly saw him as a stranger might. The light glinted off his thick white hair and wire rimmed glasses. His quiet dignity caused the entire auditorium to fall silent.

"I am especially pleased we are able to present this scholarship now, in this time of peace. My son went to war because he felt it was the right thing to do. He harboured no hatred in his heart. Just the week before last, a German submarine surrendered not far from here. And I had to ask myself, why should those men live when my son died? It isn't an easy question. Those men, who made the war so dangerous for all of us, who took the lives of those we loved, how will we treat them in the years to come? After the First World War, we were harsh with Germany. That war was so terrible, our losses so great, it seemed only right to make the Germans pay. Now, we can see how wrong we were. The broken state of Germany became the breeding ground of Nazism. Our hatred was delivered back to us tenfold.

"I hope we will learn from what has happened and stop this cycle of hatred. And I hope, as well, that the recipient of this scholarship will use his knowledge of engineering to enhance our new peace, to help us learn to beat our swords into ploughshares and put this horrible time behind us."

When he finished, there was silence. For a long moment, Ev was afraid that her grandfather's words were too hard for the audience to accept. Then, like a clap of thunder, the room burst into applause. Peter stood, clapping, and so did all the other people in the huge auditorium. That's what Grandpa tried to tell me, Ev thought, the night Joe Clouter came.

When everyone was finally silent and seated again, Miss Carlyle, headmistress at their junior school, stood to announce the winner. Ev held her breath. Let it be Peter, she thought.

"I am pleased to present the first ever Duncan McCallum

Memorial Scholarship for Studies in Engineering at McGill University to Peter Tilley," Miss Carlyle said.

There was another burst of applause. Stan leaned over to congratulate Peter. Ev could see what it cost him to be so sportsmanlike. Peter rose and accepted the congratulations, but he looked dazed rather than happy.

After, in the hall, Letty Winsor wasted no time. "So, Evelyn, you didn't win that scholarship after all."

Ev didn't feel like defending herself. "You know what, Letty? I'm happy Peter Tilley won."

That silenced her at least. Pansy Green stood nearby, listening. She should look happier than that, Ev thought. Perhaps she's sad because Peter will be away in Montreal.

The rest of the day was a trial. Ev knew how to bear the malice of her enemies. It was the sympathy of girls who liked her that rankled. Pansy remained quiet in a distracted way that puzzled Ev.

When school was finally over, Ev tried to sneak home. But Peter had stationed himself on the street where she had to pass. He did not look like someone who'd just won a scholarship. I can handle this, Ev thought. Just remain dignified and calm.

"Evelyn McCallum," he said, "I got half a mind to hand that scholarship right back to that committee. What makes you think I needs your charity?"

That did it. "You think I took myself out of the running for you? Are you cracked?"

Peter was taken aback. He paused. "Well, was it for Stan?"

"Just because I'm a girl, you think I'm going to step aside? I didn't give that scholarship up. I withdrew because I don't want to be an engineer. I think I want to be a doctor."

"A doctor?"

"Yes. Like my grandfather. Like John Thorne. Like my father wanted to be." And, before she could stop herself, Ev told Peter her grandfather's story. "So, when Ian was injured, and I helped John, I knew that's what I was good at. Just like your Nan when she was left alone and had to deliver that baby. Exactly the same."

"At the exam, when you didn't show, I thought you only did it out of pity for me," Peter said.

"I don't pity you, Peter," Ev said. I pity myself, she thought.

"Does Stan know?"

"Stan doesn't know anything. We aren't exactly friends any more." It hurt to admit this, but Peter might as well know. As soon as the girls got a hold of it, everyone would. As long as I'm embarrassing myself, Ev thought, I might as well do a good job. "Since we're playing twenty questions, maybe you'll answer one. Why are you avoiding me? Don't pretend you didn't visit Ian in the hospital, because I know you did."

Peter blushed. "I only went when I knew you wouldn't be there. I asked Nan not to tell."

"You should know her better than that. She didn't. Ian did."

"Ian? He's after growing up."

"Well, thanks to me, he almost didn't. But that's another story. Tell me what's going on, Peter. Please." Now that the edge was off her anger, Ev heard herself begin to plead. This is where I make a complete fool of myself, she thought.

Peter paused for an agonizingly long moment. Then he said, "It started at that dance at Bishop Feild College. I looked at you that night, your hair streeling down into your eyes, in that funny dress, and then I looked at Pansy Green."

Ev winced. This was going to hurt more than she'd imagined.

Peter went on. "Now, Pansy's got to be the prettiest girl in this school. And she's kind and sweet—"

That was enough. "Look, Peter, you don't have to explain. I'm sorry I asked." She began to walk past him.

But he grabbed her by the arm and held fast. "You asked me a question," he said. "Now listen while I tells you." He had a strange look in his eye that almost frightened Ev. This was not the Peter she knew.

"So I looked at Pansy that night," he continued, "and I thought to myself, what a lucky fellow I am. Anyone would want to be in my place. Then I realized there's only one thing wrong with Pansy." He paused, forcing her to ask.

"And what would that be?" Ev said. She looked at the ground. She just wanted this to end so she could crawl away and cry.

Peter relaxed his grip on her arm. "She's not you."

Ev raised her eyes. "What did you say?"

"God knows why I feels this way about you Evelyn, but I do. I have for as long as I've known you. And I knew you never loved me back. Knew you were gone on Stan Dawe, so I didn't even try. The perfect cripple. That's what I've been trying to be.

"But when I saw you that night, I knew I was through. I couldn't pretend not to feel jealous of Stan. And, as sweet and lovely as Pansy is, I couldn't pretend I might love her. We're still partners in chemistry, but that's all. So now you knows why I'm not your friend any more. I had to see Ian in the hospital, but I didn't want to be just friends with you, and I still don't."

"Still don't what?" Ev said. She wasn't sure what Peter was saying.

"I still don't want to be just friends," Peter said.

"So, does that mean you'd consider...other options?"

"What do you mean?"

Ev could hardly bear this. It was so humiliating. "I mean, you know, more than friends." She couldn't look at Peter.

"You mean us? More than friends?" The idea seemed to astonish him.

After all I've put him though, Ev thought, it would. She couldn't stand it any longer. "Never mind," she said. "I've been so foolish, and now it's too late." She turned for home before he could see the tears.

"Wait! No, it's not."

Ev stopped. "It isn't?"

"I don't think so. Come here."

She came back. He put his hands on her shoulders and kissed her, tentatively, on the lips. Right there on LeMarchant Road. Ev imagined shock behind the lace curtains across the street. She didn't care.

Peter smiled. "I wouldn't say it's too late," he said gently. "Would you?"

"I wouldn't say so either." She ran her fingertips over his cheekbone as if she was discovering his face for the first time. "I can't even remember falling in love with you," she said.

He laughed. "I'm not surprised."

"Why?"

"I think we bonded at the molecular level."

She laughed with him, an easy laugh that made her feel

this new awkwardness would quickly pass. She leaned forward and pressed her cheek into his jacket. He hesitated, then, as if gaining confidence, held her. His heartbeat didn't sound as calm as his voice. She recalled what Mrs. Bursey had said. "The heart has a mind of its own."

She looked up at him. "You know, I think Ian would like to see you."

He smiled. "I'd like to see him myself."

Historical Note

Five *Sorbus intermedia brouwers*, or Swedish mountain ash, grow on Military Road in St. John's. They shelter the monument erected to the memory of Frederick Weston Carter from the winds of the open sea. If you look, you can still see the trunk of a sixth tree, which must have died. I do not know when or why they were planted.

Between the time the war ended, and the day the terms of union with Canada were signed in 1949, the future of Newfoundland and Labrador was the subject of heated debate. Merchants like Stan Dawe's family were mainly opposed to confederation with Canada. People who lived in outports, like Pansy Green's family, were mostly in favour. But the question divided families and friends. Finally, after two referenda, 52.34 percent of the people of Newfoundland and Labrador voted to join Canada.

Most of St. John's South Side neighbourhood was demolished in 1959 to make way for new harbour developments that never quite materialized. This place is remembered in loving detail by Helen Porter in her book *Below the Bridge*.